DIFFUSED

A Shear Disaster Mystery
(Book Four)

by

Terri Reid

DIFFUSED

A Shear Disaster Mystery
(Book Four)
by
Terri Reid

The author would like to thank all those who have contributed to the creation of this book: Andrew Reid, Richard Reid, Ruth Ann Mulnix, Mickey Claus, and Terrie Snyder. And especially to the wonderful readers who are starting this whole new adventure with me, thank you all!

Chapter One

"So?" Kyle asked as he entered the back room and placed the used dye brushes and mixing bowls in the sink next to the counter where I was standing. His hands were still covered with black rubber gloves, and he was wearing a black apron over his clothes.

"So what?" I asked as I measured a little more color into the highlight dye I was mixing.

Kyle switched on the tap and turned to me while hot water ran over the things in the sink. "So, how are you holding up?" he asked.

I shrugged. "I'm fine," I lied. "I mean it's Monday, so I'm supposed to have weekend lag."

"Oh, honey, what you are experiencing is not weekend lag," he argued, as he scrubbed the bowls under the running water. "Weekend lag is when we go bargain hunting at all of the sample sales, then we head to Central

1

Park for a jog, then we get dressed up and spend the night clubbing. That's what causes weekend lag. But going to two funerals, having a good friend die, and being attacked by a demon..." Then he turned and shook his finger at me. "Oh, no, that's something else altogether."

I sighed and measured another color into another bowl for the base hair dye. "Sometimes I feel like Clark Kent," I said.

"What?" Kyle replied, meticulously cleaning the dye from the brushes. "No, girl, you are not Clark Kent. You are more like Catwoman." Then he pawed the air between us. "Meow. Much sexier."

I snorted, then shook my head. "No, I don't mean it that way," I explained. "I mean, Clark Kent was this glasses-wearing, mild-mannered, slightly uptight reporter who was always dashing away to a phone booth so he could transform in order to fight for truth, justice, and the American way. But no one knew that he was doing all that stuff behind the scenes, and he still was supposed to meet his deadlines. No matter what."

"I don't know if I'm understanding you," Kyle replied.

"During the day I'm a mild-mannered, hairstyling, salon-owning, fairly normal millennial," I explained. "But, in real life, I'm a ghost-seeing, murder-witnessing, psychic-power-wielding, nervous wreck." I sighed. "And, furthermore, you can't even find a phone booth anymore if you wanted one."

Kyle nodded slowly, turned off the water, and picked up a towel to dry the bowls. "First, you were never mild-mannered and, really honey, you…normal…I don't think so," he teased as he stacked the color bowl onto the shelf above the sink. "But I get what you're saying. So, why live the lie? Why not tell the girls what you're going through?"

"Sure," I said, as I rolled my eyes. "Ladies, I'd just like you all to know that I can see ghosts and a demon is trying to kill me and I've been peripherally involved in several murders in town."

Kyle shrugged. "Works for me."

"You're kidding, right?"

Kyle sighed and leaned against the sink. "Girl, with all you've got going on, you need to know who your friends are and who your enemies are," he said. "These ladies, here at the salon, they are your friends." Then he shook his head. "No, they are your sisters. They would do anything for you."

I thought about it for a moment. Thought about these women who worked side-by-side with me almost every day of the week, who warned me away from Ridge, and covered for me when they thought I wasn't feeling well. Who had been my momma's best friends and confidants for years.

I nodded slowly.

"You're right," I agreed. "But I don't know if I want them to be pulled into all of this mess."

"Did you ever think that just working here, working with you, is already pulling them into the mess?" he asked.

4

My eyes widened and my stomach dropped. "You mean I've put them all in danger?"

"Girl, when are you going to stop taking all the blame for the situation you're in?" he asked with exasperation. "You are not putting them in danger. But could they be in danger? Yeah, they could. Especially if you don't trust them enough to tell them the truth."

"Maybe you're right."

"Excuse me? Maybe? You are doubting my rightness?"

"What?" Ida exclaimed, entering the back room with a pile of folded towels from the laundry area. "You're white?"

Kyle grinned at me, then turned to Ida. "I said rightness, sweetie, not whiteness," he corrected her. "No offense, but brown sugar is much tastier than the plain white stuff."

Ida nodded. "And chocolate frosting is much better than vanilla," she agreed. "Well, you know, except on carrot cake. But then, I like a good cream cheese

5

frosting on carrot cake." She thought about that for a moment. "But that doesn't make as good an analogy, does it?"

"No, but I love cream cheese frosting too," Kyle agreed, his grin widening.

Then he turned to me. "Well?"

What the hell, in for a penny in for a pound!

"Ida," I said, my mind made up. "Can you schedule a team meeting for all of us this week? Maybe we could close down for a couple of hours and order lunch in."

Ida smiled and nodded. "Your momma used to do that every so often," she said. "She called them "Appreciation Lunches" and we all just loved them!"

"Well, I think it's high time we got a little appreciation around here," Kyle added. "I wonder if that place in Biloxi delivers."

Ida's eyes widened. "Well, I could run in there beforehand and pick up," she offered. "I don't mind at all."

"Perfect," I agreed. "You take the orders and then take enough money from the cash register to cover the food and your gas."

"You know," Ida mused excitedly. "I bet I could arrange it for today, if y'all don't mind a late lunch."

"That works for me," Kyle agreed.

"See if that works for everyone else," I replied, feeling better about this idea by the minute. "And don't forget desserts."

"That's the best part of any meal," Ida agreed, hurrying to the door. "I'll let y'all know as soon as I can."

Once she was gone, Kyle turned back to me. "Nice going Clark," he said with a wink. "Time to rip off those glasses."

I nodded. "Yes, it is."

Chapter Two

"Now, tell me all about what's going on in your life," the prim octogenarian demanded as I brushed the bright red hair dye onto her short locks.

Miss Marylou Young had been my third-grade teacher, my momma's third-grade teacher, my daddy's third-grade teacher, and probably the third-grade teacher for most of the population of Julep, Mississippi.

The school district finally forced her to retire when she was seventy-five, and she never forgave them for that decision. To get even, the petite, red-headed dynamo got elected to be the representative of the local teacher's union and takes them all back to school every year when it's time to renegotiate the contracts.

I adjusted a hair clip and started working on the second level of roots. "Well, you know," I said. "Running the salon, now that Momma's gone, has been an adjustment."

"I can tell you, Louella Jo, that she would be mighty proud of what you're doing," Miss Marylou said.

"Thank you," I replied. "That means a lot to me."

"Although," she added with a sniff. "I'm still not too sure about these blonde highlights. Are you sure they won't make me look old?"

I bit back the smile and met her eyes through the mirror. "Actually, the lighter color around your face will make you look younger," I said. "It will soften the lines…"

"Lines?" she interrupted me, but I could see the laughter in her eyes. "Are you insinuating that I have wrinkles?"

I grinned back. "No ma'am," I quickly replied. "I was referring to contouring lines of your face."

She chuckled softly. "As I recall, you were a storyteller way back in third grade, weren't you?"

"Is that a polite way of calling me a liar?" I asked as I prepared the first foil.

"I would never call the person who has my hair's future in the literal palms of her hands a liar," she teased. "Now, your Momma, however, there was a person who could spin a yarn with the best of them."

Laughing, I nodded. "Yes, my momma had quite a talent for prevaricating."

Miss Marylou raised her eyebrows and winked at me. "Prevaricating? Well, that's a bonus word from your spelling list."

"Do you want me to use it in a sentence?" I asked as I folded up another foil near her forehead.

"I believe you just did," she replied.

"Do I get a gold star?" I asked.

"Let's wait and see how my hair turns out first," she teased.

"Oh, you are going to want to give me two gold stars when you see it," I assured her, really enjoying the conversation. I wasn't nearly as intimidated as I thought I'd be when I'd first seen her name on the schedule.

"Hmmm, it seems that New York City might have given you an overinflated sense of confidence," she quipped.

Okay, maybe I still was a little intimidated.

"She was always a bully," Momma said, appearing next to me. "Don't let her get to you. I tried to talk her into highlights for years and she always turned me down. Seems to me, she respects you more than she lets on."

I sent Momma a doubtful glance and she grinned. "Go on, meet her bluff and see what happens," she said. "I think you'll be surprised."

I took a deep breath and nodded. "No, New York didn't give me an overinflated sense of confidence, it just helped me realize that I was good at what I did," I replied, then I grinned at her. "You know, if you can make it there, you can make it anywhere."

She actually chuckled. "That was clever," she said with a nod of approval. "And I am now leaning toward being excited about the big reveal."

I finished folding up the last foil and tucked it neatly into place. Then I covered her head with a black plastic cap and wiped a bit of dye from her ear. "Okay, you need to let everything process for about 30 minutes," I said as I picked up the nearly empty bowls of color. "Can I get you a magazine or a bottle of water?"

"A bottle of water would be lovely," Miss Marylou replied. "And I brought a book along because I knew I'd have to wait." She held up her tablet and pointed to the black and white book cover. The author's name seemed familiar, but I couldn't place her.

"Is it a good story?" I asked.

"So far," she replied. "It's a paranormal mystery about a former Chicago policewoman who can see ghosts and becomes a private detective so she can help solve their murders, so they can move on to the light." She rolled her eyes. "Ghosts - totally unbelievable, but it's fun reading."

I nodded and pursed my lips for a moment. "Right," I finally said, sending a surreptitious wink to Momma. "Totally unbelievable. I'll get you that water."

12

Chapter Three

"I have never seen Miss Marylou smile like that," Ida said, just before she bit off the top half of a piece of shrimp. "She kept glancing in every mirror she passed. Couldn't get enough of her new do."

We had flipped the sign to "CLOSED," passed around Styrofoam take-out boxes with each individual order, and we were perched either in salon chairs or had pulled the extra chairs in from the break room so we could sit in a circle in the middle of the salon.

"We should do this every day," Georgia sighed, after sipping on her extra-large diet soda. "We deserve this."

"Well, I won't argue that we deserve this," Maribelle agreed. "But eating like this every day would diminish the profits and expand our waistlines."

"You know," Ida began. "I watched this special on tv about how they inject shrimp..."

"No! No! No!" Kasey shouted. "I do not want to have this moment spoiled by a documentary." She waved her piece of shrimp in the air. "All I want to know is that this is a deep-fried object of deliciousness."

Ida chuckled. "Well, it was Chinese shrimp any who," she replied. "Not Gulf shrimp. And the fellow…"

She stopped when the front door opened and turned her chair to face it. "I'm sorry," she called. "We're not…"

She paused when Van poked his head around the door. "I heard there was a meeting," he said. "With food."

My stomach was suddenly filled with nerves, and I felt my skin grow warm. Just Van's presence did crazy things to my equilibrium. Which is why I'd decided not to invite him.

I glared at Kyle, who widened his eyes in supposed innocence and then shrugged.

"Well, come on in, good-looking," Ida called to him. "You want some shrimp?"

Van securely closed the door behind him, strolled to just inside the counter, and smiled at the group. "Well, I heard that this was going to be a laying-the-cards on the table kind of meeting," he said with a smile.

"Really?" Maribelle replied, glancing from Van to me. "What kind of cards you got up your sleeve?"

Van grinned at her and nodded. "I'm glad you asked," he said, then he sauntered in my direction.

Did I say saunter? No, it was more like stalked. He was doing that whole Southern panther thing again, his eyes totally focused on mine. My heart was pounding in my chest.

He wasn't going to try and kiss me, was he?

For heaven's sakes, I have shrimp breath.

But he just moved in and swooped down.

His lips touched mine and I shivered. He coaxed and teased my lips until I opened under him with a soft moan so he could taste me fully. The salon disappeared. The world disappeared. All that mattered was this amazing man who held me in his arms.

15

Moments passed, minutes passed, or hours passed – I had no idea - all I knew was that my bones were melted and my senses were foggy. Van slowly lifted his head, tenderly smiled down at me, and then turned to the rest of the group. "Cards on the table," he said, his voice slightly hoarse with emotion. "I am totally, completely, hopelessly in love with L.J."

I think the room exploded in catcalls and shouts of congratulations, but I barely heard them.

Stunned.

That's the only word I can think of that comes even close to how I was feeling. Van had said the "l-word" twice in two days and I hadn't had the nerve to even say it once.

I turned to him, fearing a look of anticipation on his face. Afraid that he was waiting for me to say the same thing. And why the heck wouldn't he expect it? That's what you do, right?

But he wasn't even looking at me. He was looking at Kyle.

16

"I got your order, man," Kyle was saying, holding up an extra Styrofoam container. "Ribs, right?"

"Right," Van replied, walking away from me, and moving toward Kyle who was sitting in the chair under the big hairdryer. "Thanks."

Van took a seat next to Kyle, under the other big hairdryer, and opened up his container. Then he glanced up at me and grinned. "The shrimp tasted good," he said with a wink. "But I prefer the ribs."

I was totally confused. And I really wanted to run away, just to clear my head.

I closed the lid on my container, put it on the counter next to my chair, and stood up. "I just need a minute," I said, then I hurried to the back room.

Chapter Four

I closed the door of the office and leaned against the door. I didn't want anyone following me. I just needed to be alone.

"Louella Jo Carter," Momma said, appearing in front of me.

I sighed. Why is it what you need and what you get are so often polar opposites?

"Don't scold me, Momma," I said, trying to keep the quiver out of my voice. "I don't think I could take it."

"Why in the world would I scold you?" she asked.

"Because I might have hurt Van's feelings in the worst possible way and in front of a room full of people," I replied, the words rushing out in a sob.

"Did you mean to hurt him?" she asked.

Tears slipping down my cheeks, I impatiently brushed them away, and shook my head. "No, of course not," I cried. "I just don't understand..."

"Why you can't say it back?" she asked.

I nodded.

"Do you? Do you love Van?"

I nodded again. "Oh, yes, I know I do," I whispered. "I've never…"

"You've never felt like this before?" she finished for me.

"Right," I agreed, moving from the door to my wheeled, office chair next to the desk. "Never felt so many emotions at the same time. Joy, passion, excitement, fear, anxiety…"

"Those last two don't sound like they fit," she said, perplexed.

There was a soft knock on the door.

"Oh, Momma," I said. "I just can't talk to Van right now. I just can't…"

"L.J., it's me, Kyle," Kyle whispered from the other side of the door. "Can I come in?"

I sighed and nodded. Momma opened the door and let him come in.

19

"Are you okay?" he asked, pulling up a chair and sitting next to me.

I shook my head. "I am such a big jerk," I replied. "I should have immediately told everyone that I loved Van too."

He nodded. "Is it true?" he asked.

"Yes. I know it is," I said earnestly. "There is no doubt in my mind…"

I couldn't face him. I couldn't face anyone. So, I rolled my chair toward the wall and tried to blot up all the tears running down my face.

"So, why do you think…" Momma began to ask.

"I know," Kyle said, stopping Momma's question.

He reached over and placed his hands on my shoulders and turned me back to face him. "How many people in your life have you felt this kind of love for?"

I shrugged. "Well, you know I love you and I love…"

He shook his head. "No, sweetie, you and I both know the kind of love we share is friendship love," he replied. "Which is amazing, but it's not the kind of love that destroys us if we lose it."

My eyes suddenly overflowed with tears as the truth of what he was saying touched something deep inside of me.

"How many?" he asked.

"Two," I wept softly. "Two people."

"Your momma and your daddy, right?"

I nodded, my throat too tight to say the words.

He reached over to my desk and pulled out another tissue and wiped the tears away. "And what happened to both of those people?" he asked.

The trickle of tears became a waterfall. "They left me. They died," I cried.

"And why don't you want to say I love you to Van?" he asked gently.

I finally understood. "Because I don't want him to die," I whispered.

"Well, that's a relief," Van said from the doorway.

I gasped, then spun around in my chair. "I didn't...I don't...I..." I stammered.

"Can we have a moment?" he asked Kyle and Momma.

Kyle winked at me, then got up and walked past Van, closing the door behind him.

Momma bent over, kissed my forehead, and then disappeared.

Van stood next to the door for a few moments while I wiped away the tears and tried to compose myself. "Are we okay?" he asked.

I nodded.

He pushed himself away from the door, walked to my desk, and took the chair Kyle had vacated. "I didn't mean to upset you," he said softly. "Actually, I wasn't planning on doing what I did until I walked into the salon and saw you sitting there." He plucked another tissue from the box and wiped some remaining tears from my cheeks. "I just had to tell the world how much I loved you."

I smiled. It was a watery smile, but it was a start.

"You didn't upset me," I explained. "I upset me. I should have told everyone how I felt, right after you did. But it just wouldn't come out."

"But not because you don't love me," he stated.

"No," I said, meeting his eyes and praying that he could see both the truth and the love in mine. "But because I was afraid."

"I get that," he said. "And, you know, you're dealing with a lot right now. So, when you are ready to say it. I'll be ready to hear it."

He leaned forward and kissed me gently on the lips. "I'm a patient man, L.J.," he whispered. "And your declaration of love is worth waiting for."

"But you know...you understand..."

He kissed me again.

"Yeah, I do," he replied. "But I still want to hear you say it someday."

"I will," I said, hoping that I wasn't lying. "I will someday."

Chapter Five

I was prepared for things to be really awkward when we walked out of the back room and into the main salon. I wasn't sure how I was going to explain myself and I certainly did not want all the ladies to get the wrong impression about my feelings for Van.

So, I really wasn't prepared to have Ida rush towards me, tears slipping down her cheeks, and enfold me in her plump arms. "It's okay," she sobbed, patting my back with gentle reassurance. "It's okay."

"Thank you," I replied, more than a little confused.

Ida stepped back, wiped the tears from her cheeks, and then blew her nose, loudly. "Kyle explained it all," she said through a watery smile. "We all understand."

"Oh, well, that was so nice of Kyle," I replied, sending him a frantic look.

"We all know how much you loved your momma," Kyle said pointedly. "And when Van declared himself and you just wished your momma were alive and could be here with all of us to hear those words. Well, we all understand how your emotions just got the best of you and you needed a moment alone."

Have I mentioned how much I love Kyle?

"Thank you, Kyle," I said, linking my arm through Van's arm. "It's so nice to have friends who are understanding." Then I turned to Van. "And it's a wonderful thing to fall in love."

There was a chorus of soft exclamations from the ladies. But Van leaned close to me and whispered, "Yeah, that doesn't count."

I chuckled softly. "That's what I figured," I whispered back.

We made our way back to our chairs and our meals. Van sat next to Kyle, and I took my place back on the styling chair. "Well, I did have something else I needed to talk to you about today," I said.

"What's on your mind?" Maribelle asked.

"Well, since I've been home, some things have changed in my life," I began.

Ida started sobbing again.

I turned in her direction. "Oh, honey, no. I didn't mean that," I exclaimed. Then I shrugged. "Well, in a way I did mean or do mean that."

Ida patted her eyes with a fresh tissue. "I don't understand," she said.

"When I came home from New York, Bea met me at the airport," I explained. "She sat down next to me on the bus and told me that my momma had sent her to meet me."

"But your momma was dead," Kasey said, shaking her head. "How could she send Bea?"

"Right!" I replied. "And I have to admit, at first I thought Bea was some kind of con artist or some crazy person."

Van chuckled and then tried to hide it behind a cough.

"Then she told me that she was psychic, and my momma's ghost had come to her," I explained. "And then I thought she was crazy for sure."

"We have a ghost at our place," Georgia said casually, as she scooped up a forkful of coleslaw. "I've seen him in the back, by the barn. Young fellow, wearing a Confederate soldier's uniform."

A chill swept down my back and I nodded. "Then you will understand when I tell you that when I got home that night, Momma's ghost appeared to me."

There was a moment of stunned silence, then Maribelle nodded. "I thought I'd seen her here at the salon," she said. "I catch a quick glimpse out of the corner of my eye."

"Yes, she's been here all right," I said.

"Why? Why is she still here?" Ida asked. "Your momma was one of the sweetest ladies I've ever known. She didn't have any unfinished business."

"Well, actually, she did," I said. "Momma didn't die of natural causes. Momma was murdered."

27

Chapter Six

"Murdered?" Ida gasped, shaking her head vehemently. "No! Why would anyone want to kill your momma?"

"JoEllen Carlisle," Maribelle stated bluntly. "It had to be something with JoEllen and her disappearance. Right?"

Why had I ever thought that these ladies couldn't handle the truth?

"Right," I confirmed. "They thought Momma had information about the folks who killed her."

"And did she?" Maribelle asked.

"Well, not that she knew of at the time," I replied.

"So, who do we got to kill?" Kasey asked.

"Kasey!" Georgia scolded, then she lowered her voice. "You don't know if this place is bugged or not." She glanced over at me and whispered. "So, who do we got to kill?"

This might sound a little weird to y'all, but the amount of love I had for these ladies at this moment was pretty near overwhelming. I shook my head, and then bent my head in Van's direction. "He's a former Special Agent for the FBI," I whispered.

All eyes turned on Van for a long moment.

"Van, honey, you want to leave the room?" Maribelle requested.

"No, I do not," Van replied emphatically. "Y'all are not going to kill anyone. Do you understand?"

"Oh, sure, we understand," Georgia said, sending me a hidden wink. "We were all just funning. Right girls?"

Ida shook her head, looking very confused. "It didn't sound like we were funning," she exclaimed.

Maribelle rolled her eyes. "I'll explain it to you later, honey," she said.

"Well, it didn't," Ida muttered.

"Can I just say that I am so glad all you ladies are on my side," Kyle inserted. "I mean, we went from

Momma's a ghost to who we gotta kill in record time. Are y'all part of some Southern ladies' crime syndicate?"

"Yes, we are," Kasey replied evenly. "The Southern Mississippi Beauticians Association. We specialize in curl up and dye."

I snorted. It wasn't a pretty sound, but it just kind of came out and suddenly all eyes turned back to me.

"You say something?" Kyle asked, knowing full well that I hadn't.

"I think we need to get back on track, here," I replied. "I didn't tell you about Momma's murder so you could all form a hit squad and take someone out, though from the bottom of my heart I appreciate the sentiment." I clapped my hands over my heart in a gesture of pure appreciation, then I slowly looked around the room at each of them. "I needed to tell you in case there is any danger, so you can protect yourselves?"

"What kind of danger?' Maribelle asked.

"Well, so far, since I've been home, three people have died in my presence," I said.

30

"Dang girl," Georgia said. "Who the hell have you been hanging around with?"

Maribelle slowly shook her head. "I can guess two," she said. "We all know about Sheriff King, right?"

I nodded.

"Okay, that's one," Maribelle continued. "I'm guessing that Patterson boy...Ridge. I'm guessing he's one of them too."

"How did you..." I began.

Maribelle shrugged. "That boy was sniffing around your skirt like a tomcat," she explained. "And the fact that the same night he died, the sheriff died on your front lawn? Yeah, that was way too coincidental."

"You work for the FBI too?" Kyle asked her.

Maribelle smiled. "Naw, but I've been doing hair for a couple of decades here and you sure learn a lot about people when you do hair," she said. Then she turned to me. "The last one. I can't rightly put my finger on that one."

31

"Could be because no one knows he's dead yet," I explained, then I paused for a moment and slowly looked around the room. "And if anyone finds out that we know, we could all be in a lot of trouble."

"My lips are sealed," Maribelle said, then she turned to Ida. "I know you can keep a secret. But if you think something might slip out, you might want to go to the ladies' room for a minute."

Ida shook her head. "I know I can be silly at times," she said. "But I need to be part of this. I want to be part of this. I want to help."

A montage of Ida's slip-of-the-tongue incidents ran through my mind, and I admit that I was hesitant to share the information about Deputy Hill.

Ida noticed my hesitation and nodded sadly. "I don't blame you at all," she said graciously, as she slipped from her chair and began to walk toward the back of the salon. "Why don't y'all just let me know when you're ready for me."

Chapter Seven

"Wait," I called after her. "I need you to hear this too, Ida. I need *all* the people I trust to hear this."

She turned, her eyes bright with tears, and nodded. "Thank you," she whispered. "Ain't no one ever going to hear none of this from my lips." She drew a cross over her ample chest with her finger. "Cross my heart and hope to die."

"I know, Ida," I replied. "I know I can trust you and I know my momma trusted you."

"That was well-done of you," Momma said, as she appeared next to me. "Ida has a heart of gold. She might be silly, but she's not stupid. You trusting her, well, she's gonna be loyal to you for life."

I took a deep breath and nodded. "A few nights after Momma's funeral, I got a call in the middle of the night," I explained. "The caller said that he knew how my momma had died. He wanted me to meet him at the beach and he would give me the information."

"And you immediately called the police, right?" Maribelle asked.

"Right?!?!?" Kyle inserted, nodding his head enthusiastically. "Or she could have immediately awakened her houseguest who would have come with her to the beach."

"Exactly," Maribelle agreed.

I rolled my eyes and shook my head. "This isn't about what I could have or should have done," I said. "It's about what I did and what happened."

Kyle folded his arms across his chest and snorted. "Well, I'm just saying, I'm not the only one who thought you shouldn't have gone alone. For the record."

"Fine, for the record," I agreed. "Next time, I will wake you up."

"Next time, you'll call me," Van added.

I sighed loudly. "Yes, fine, next time, I will wake Kyle up and call you," I said, exasperated. "Now, can I continue?"

Kasey raised her hand.

"Yes, Kasey," I replied.

"You can call me too," she offered. "I don't live too far from the beach. I could meet you there."

"If Buddy ain't fighting a fire, I could come too," Georgia added. "I took a self-defense class down by the Y, and I was pretty darn good if I say so myself."

Yes, I had totally lost control of my own meeting.

I glanced over at Van and he had the audacity to grin at me. I had to bite my cheek to keep from smiling back.

"Okay," I said, raising my voice over the cacophony of voices offering to help. "I will send out a group text to y'all should the situation ever arise again. I promise."

Just so you know, I did have my fingers crossed behind my back when I said that. But, it did the trick, the noise died down.

"So, I went down to the beach, in the middle of the night, with no one else for backup," I said quickly.

"And Deputy Hill was there. With a gun. I figured he was planning on killing me."

The communal gasp was almost funny. Almost, if I hadn't suddenly remembered how terrified I was at the time.

"It was a stupid thing to do," I said, my voice shaking just a little bit. "And I really thought that I was going to pay for my stupidity."

"What happened?" Maribelle asked. "I haven't seen Deputy Hill around for ages."

"Someone shot him," I answered.

"Who?" Ida asked.

"I don't know," I said. "They were in a boat, offshore."

"Luckily you didn't get killed too," Georgia said.

I sighed and nodded. "Well, honestly, I might have if Van hadn't come along and got me out of target range," I confessed.

"Van saved you?" Georgia asked, turning to Van and winking. "Now, ain't that romantic?"

"How'd ya know?" Ida asked Van. "Did you get some intuition that only people in love get?"

Van shook his head. "No, Bea woke me up and told me to hightail it to the beach because L.J.'s momma had told her that L.J. had gone to the beach by herself."

"See, even your momma knew you shouldn't have gone," Maribelle added.

"But I ain't heard nothing about Deputy Hill being killed," Kasey said.

"Right," I agreed, grateful to have the conversation move from me to him. "No one has reported him dead. And the fellow from the Mississippi Bureau of Investigations…"

"You mean that hunky trooper?" Georgia asked. "I kept hoping he was a stripper-gram."

"Oh girl, you and me both," Kyle said.

"He is investigating Deputy Hill's disappearance and Sheriff King's death," I replied.

"And you didn't tell anyone about this beach encounter?" Maribelle asked.

I shook my head. "Well, just you all and the Book Club," I said. "I mean, who else can I trust?"

"You can trust us," Ida said emphatically.

"Can you trust that trooper fellow?" Maribelle asked. "Seems like you were old friends."

I shrugged. "I don't know," I confessed. "He's a member of the Sons of Mississippi, so I'm not sure where his loyalties lie."

"So, what do you need us to do?" Maribelle asked.

"Right," Georgia added. "What's the next step."

"We could go undercover," Ida suggested.

I shook my head, as an absurd image of Ida in a trench coat flashed in my mind. "No. No, I don't want you to do anything," I said. "I wanted to tell you, so you can protect yourselves and so you know when crazy things happen...well, you'll know why."

"No," Kasey said.

Confused, I stared at Kasey for a long moment. "What?" I asked.

"No," Kasey repeated. "We are not just going to protect ourselves. We are going to help you, whether you like it or not. We're family."

"Damn right," Maribelle added.

I felt tears build up behind my eyes and, for a moment, I couldn't use my voice. I just nodded and wiped away the few escapees that trailed down my cheeks. "Thank you," I whispered. "Thank you."

Ida glanced up at the clock and then back at the group. "Well, we have time for one group hug before the clients start showing up," she said, her voice as watery as mine felt. "So, we better make it quick."

Chapter Eight

"Well, that was quite a day," Kyle said. He was sitting in his chair with his shoes off, giving himself a foot massage while I put together the deposit for the bank.

"It certainly was an emotional rollercoaster," I agreed. "You were right for suggesting I share with the ladies. They were amazing."

He looked up and grinned. "Amazing doesn't begin to describe it," he laughed. "They were ready to fight someone for you. No, kill someone for you." His face sobered. "They are good friends."

I shook my head. "No, they're family," I said, then I smiled at him. "And you are the crazy brother."

"The sexy, stylish, well-groomed, and buff gay brother, right?" he asked.

"Don't forget humble," I teased, as I put the money in the deposit envelope.

"Oh, honey, when you are as amazing as I am, it's hard to be humble," he replied with a smile. "So, what's up for tonight?"

"Are you talking about food?" I asked, surprised because I was still full from lunch.

"Oh, no, I couldn't eat another thing," he replied, then he paused for a moment. "Well, you know, maybe some of that leftover dessert."

"We have leftover dessert?" I asked, maybe I wasn't as full as I thought.

He chuckled. "I hid some in the fridge, behind the almond milk that no one ever uses," he confessed. "I figured we'd need some extra carbs tonight."

"Well, I'm just about ready," I said. "So, if you want to bag them up, I'll write the deposit slip, and then we can go."

A few minutes later, with the salon locked up and the desserts in a small cooler in the car, Kyle and I were standing in line at the bank, waiting behind half a dozen other business owners who were depositing their day's earnings too.

"How about a movie tonight," Kyle suggested.

"Sounds great," I replied. "Which one?"

"*Steel Magnolias*," Kyle suggested.

The woman in line just in front of us, who owned the antique store two blocks from the salon, turned around and smiled. "I just love that movie," she gushed. "Who would have guessed that Dolly Parton was such a great actress?"

"Right?" Kyle said. "Of course, I loved her in *9 to 5*, she was so believable."

"Yes, she was," the woman replied. "And how about *A Smoky Mountain Christmas*?"

"With Kenny Rogers?" Kyle asked.

"Right!" the woman exclaimed.

"I loved that," Kyle exclaimed right back. "Course, you have to admit, she was just playing herself in that role."

"That's true," she said. "But those two had such chemistry."

"Well, speaking of chemistry," Kyle added. "How about Dolly and Burt Reynolds in *Best Little Whorehouse in Texas*?"

"Oh, I'd nearly forgotten about that one," the woman began. "What did you think…"

I let her voice fade into the background while I pulled out my phone and checked my emails. She and Kyle were so caught up in Dolly trivia that I knew neither one of them would care that I wasn't listening.

I scrolled through my emails, deleting most of them, and clicked on one that advertised a sale in a shop I'd frequented in New York. I'd just accessed the website and was entering my size when the bank door opened behind me. I didn't pay any attention, I figured it was just another business owner with their daily deposits. Besides, the sale was 75% off and only until midnight.

Then I heard the pump action of a shotgun being loaded and froze.

43

"Y'all put your hands in the air," the deep male

voice demanded. "This here's a bank robbery."

Chapter Nine

I spent a long enough time in New York City that I always wore my purse in front of me. I slipped the deposit envelope deeper into the purse and then raised my hands up.

Looking up, I met Kyle's eyes and was grateful to see calm assessment and not fear. He nodded slowly at me and, then also raised his hands up.

"Two," he mouthed.

So, there were two robbers.

I tilted my head to catch a glimpse of them in the overhead mirror. Both were spindly fellows, tall with not a whole lot of muscle on them. They had on black masks tied like bandanas over their mouths and noses and stocking caps pulled down low over their heads, so we really couldn't see much of their faces.

"Y'all need to lay down on the ground," the other robber yelled, his voice was higher pitched than the first.

"Naw, idiot, we need 'em to move to the sides of the room," his companion corrected him. "Else they're gonna block our way to the tellers."

"Right. Right," the higher-pitched one replied. "Okay, move to the sides of the room and keep your mouths shut!"

We started to slowly move, our hands on our heads, when suddenly, the woman who'd been chatting with Kyle started to sob hysterically. "Please, please don't kill me," she screamed. "I have children. I have grandchildren."

"Shut up!" the higher-pitched one shouted, pointing his gun at her. "Just shut up!"

Kyle subtly stepped sideways, getting in between the woman and the gun-wielding robber. "She's just frightened," he said in a calm, soothing voice. "She didn't mean anything by it."

"What? You're not frightened?" the young man snarled, changing the direction of his weapon so it was now pointed at Kyle.

46

I didn't know about Kyle, but I was scared to death. And when I looked into the gunman's eyes, I could see he was terrified too. The hand that was holding the gun was slightly shaking, and his voice was tense. But him being scared didn't ease my mind at all, because a frightened, nervous man with a gun is liable to do something stupid, really stupid, to prove he's in control.

"Well, are you?" he demanded.

Kyle nodded slowly. "Yes, I am," he said respectfully.

"Good!" the young man spat, and some of the fear seemed to leave his eyes. "You should be. You should be very afraid of me."

"Shut your damn mouth and get over here," the first robber called.

The second robber stepped backward, away from Kyle and the woman, and hurried to his partner.

"Sorry, Ja—" he began.

"Shut up," the first robber screamed. "You want them to know my name?"

The second robber shook his head. "No. No, sorry," he stammered.

Damn. Neither of them could have been much older than twenty-five and the way they were arguing, they must have been family. And by the way, they were handling things, it must have been their first time trying to rob a bank.

Those stupid boys. They were about to ruin their lives, for probably a pretty paltry sum of money. I really wished there were something I could do to make them change their minds.

As they stood together across the room, something strange happened. The air started moving, like the air above the hot pavement in the summertime, between the two robbers. Then I could see another person, an older woman, slowly materialize and stand next to them.

And I could see through her. She turned to me and smiled. "Honey, you want to help them?" she asked me.

My eyes widened in surprise.

"Dang fool boys. Their daddy didn't amount to a hill of beans and their momma up and died when they were just knee-high to a grasshopper," she explained. "They've been pretty lost since I died last winter. Ain't bad boys, just not real smart."

"What should I do?" I whispered to her.

"What?" Kyle whispered to me,

I shook my head at him and motioned to the ghost with my head.

Kyle looked in that direction and, of course, couldn't see anything.

"Ghost," I mouthed.

"Ohhhhhh," he mouthed back.

"You just tell those boys I have something to say to them," the ghost said, her arms folded over her ample chest. "And you tell them they better listen up."

Sure. Right. That will be easy.

I'm just going to tell two men with guns they better listen up.

What could possibly go wrong?

49

"Excuse me," I said.

Both men turned toward me. "We said shut up!"

I nodded slowly. "I know," I agreed, lifting my hands in surrender. "I know, but there's someone..."

"You want to die?" the younger one asked.

"No. No, I don't," I said quickly. "But there's an older woman standing next to y'all and she's trying to communicate with you."

For a moment, both of the men froze and slowly looked around. "What did you say?" the older one asked.

"There's an older woman with you," I said, then I shrugged. "Ever since my momma died, I could see things. People...who have passed."

"You saying a dead woman is with us?" the older one growled.

"She's got gray hair, up in a bun," I said. "She's heavy set, wearing what you'd call a house dress with a floral print."

"You're making this up?" the younger one said, pointing his gun at me.

"Ask me something," I said. "So, I can ask her."

"What's her name?" the older one asked.

I turned to the ghost and prayed she would answer their question.

"They want to know your name."

"They know my name," she said.

"Right, they know your name, but they can't see you," I explained. "And they don't believe you're here."

"I'm their grammy, Grammy Anderson," she said. "Thelma Anderson. Tell 'em that."

I turned to the men. "She's your grandmother, except she said grammy. Grammy Anderson."

The younger man's eyes widened. "How did she do that?" he asked, then he turned to his brother. "Remember. Remember when I said I thought I heard Grammy Anderson talking to us and you said I was hearing stuff?"

The older man shook his head. "It's a trick," he replied to his brother. "It's got to be a trick."

"I promise you," I said. "I don't like having this ability any more than you like hearing about it. But, you know, she wants to tell you something and I'm kind of obliged to deliver her message."

"We should listen," the younger brother said. "You know, just in case."

"Fine," he sneered. "What's her message."

She glided over and whispered to me, then I repeated it to the men. "She says that you are better than this. She says that you don't have to walk in your papa's footsteps, that you have brains, and you have courage, and that he was just a big, mean coward."

Kyle gasped softly and I realized what I'd just said about their father.

"I'm sorry," I quickly added. "Really, I'm just repeating..."

The look on the man's face had changed and he nodded slowly. "Yeah, I know," he said. "That's grammy talking."

"She said she has some money put away," I continued. "Said that it's enough for the lawyers you're going to need because you were stupid enough to break the law, and then some extra to buy the auto repair shop you wanted to buy. She's been trying to tell you, but you haven't been listening."

"Grammy told us there was money. Just afore she died," the younger man insisted. "No one else knew about it. Maybe she ain't lying."

The older man slowly scanned the room. "Yeah, maybe she ain't," he agreed. "I mean, how the hell would she know about Grammy?"

"So…you mean…Grammy is here?" the younger man searched around the room. "I'm sorry, Grammy."

"She says for you both to put your guns down on the ground, so the police don't shoot you," I said, although that was my suggestion, not Grammy's, and they both complied.

As soon as the guns were on the ground, to my surprise, Franklin, my own personal Mississippi Trooper, stepped out from the back room, his gun aimed at the two men. "Step away from those guns, gentlemen," he said. "And no one gets hurt."

"Where'd he come from?" the younger man asked.

Excellent question.

"The bank's alarm system was activated moments after you stepped through that door," Franklin explained, as he walked toward us. "We came in through the back door. You would have never made it out of here with the money."

"Or made it out of here alive," Kyle murmured, looking at the other troopers filing out of the back, their guns pointed at the two men.

They both looked at me. "Grammy says it will be okay," I said. "And I know a really good lawyer, I'll call him up for you."

"Thank you, ma'am," the older one said as he backed away from his gun. "Tell Grammy we're awfully sorry for disappointing her."

Grammy whispered again. "Grammy says that she loves you," I repeated. "And that you could never disappoint her. But you could make her madder than a wet hen."

Two troopers came forward, handcuffed the pair, and walked them out of the bank to the waiting squad car. I turned to Kyle and breathed a sigh of relief. "I'm so glad that's over," I said.

"Oh, it's not over," Franklin said from behind me. "It's far from being over."

Chapter Ten

"Excuse me?" I asked turning to face Franklin with more than a little attitude, because, quite frankly, I'd had enough of this day. "What do you mean by that?"

Franklin lowered his voice, so only Kyle and I could hear him. "We need to talk about what just went on here," he said. He glanced around to be sure no one was within hearing distance. "You know, about your abilities."

"Well, you can talk to her tomorrow," Kyle insisted quietly, stepping up a little into Franklin's space. "L.J. not only just saved the bank from being robbed, but she also probably saved some lives here. So, you are going to let her go home and take it easy before you even think about giving her the third degree."

"You don't tell me what I can or cannot do," Franklin replied firmly.

"Oh, you're right," Kyle said easily. "But when I raise my voice with all these witnesses in the room and demand why you are questioning the woman that saved their lives, I think you might get some unwanted press about it."

The testosterone was getting thick, and I was getting tired of being talked about like I wasn't there or couldn't make up my own mind about what was best for me. "Excuse me," I said, stepping in between the two men. "I'm tired. I'm going home after I make my deposit. Franklin, if you need to talk to me tonight, you can come over to the house in about an hour. If it can wait until tomorrow, I'd appreciate it."

Then I turned and walked away from both of them and headed over to one of the tellers, who was more than happy to take my deposit. "You were just wonderful," she gushed, as she counted the money. "It was just like on one of those TV shows where the people can talk to ghosts. I've never seen anything like it in all my born days."

"It's a little surprising to me too," I admitted.

"You said, it's been since your momma passed, right?" she asked

I nodded.

"Your momma was a fine lady," she said softly. "I miss her smile."

I nodded, tears filling my eyes. "I do too," I replied.

She typed the amounts into the computer and then printed out a receipt. Then she leaned forward and placed her hand over mine. "Your momma would have been real proud of you today," she said, finally handing me the receipt. "Real proud."

"Thank you."

I turned away from her and, to my surprise, Momma was standing right in front of me. "What the hell were you thinking?" she demanded. "It's just money. Money can be replaced; you cannot be replaced."

So much for real proud.

I glanced over at Kyle and could tell by his smirk that he had seen and heard Momma too. I looked around the lobby and saw that Franklin was busily engaged with Harold Murphy, the bank president. I smiled to myself. Just desserts, I thought. Then I made eye contact with

Kyle, angled my head in the direction of the door, and headed that way as fast as I could.

Momma followed.

"Don't you walk away from me when I'm nearly scared to death for you," she lectured as we left the bank.

"Momma, you can't be scared to death anymore," I countered. I actually thought that was a very good argument. "Besides, nothing happened."

"Nothing happened because of God's good grace," she replied. "Why didn't you have the common sense to just hush up and keep your nose out of other people's business?"

I reached the car and looked at her before I opened the car door. "Because, Momma, I have your DNA and, unfortunately, we Carter women have a problem with that."

That sure shut her mouth.

Well, until I got into the car.

"Aren't you supposed to learn from my mistakes?" she asked. "If I hadn't butted my nose into JoEllen's business…"

"Momma," I said with a sigh. "I did learn from you. I learned that caring for others doesn't just happen when it's convenient. I learned that sometimes you need to risk a little to help others. I learned that money isn't important but stopping two young men from making a mistake that will change their whole lives is." I glanced in the rearview mirror to see the tears in her eyes. "It's in my DNA, Momma. And I got it from both you and Daddy."

Momma sighed. "Fine," she finally said. "And to tell you the truth, when I wasn't terrified, I was proud. Real proud."

Chapter Eleven

As soon as I turned onto my street, I saw Van's truck parked in front of the house. "How did he know?" I asked.

"Maybe he doesn't," Kyle replied. "Maybe he just came over to get him some sugar."

Then he proceeded to make obnoxious kissy sounds.

"Are you twelve?" I asked him, although I have met some twelve-year-olds who have shown more maturity than Kyle.

He grinned. "Which would you prefer, him wanting sugar or him knowing what happened?" he asked.

I sighed. "Sugar," I agreed. Then, as I pulled into the driveway, Van dashed down porch steps toward the car, a look of concern on his face.

"This sure isn't about sugar," Kyle said quietly.

"Let's just hope he didn't hear about what really happened," I replied softly.

I turned off the car and opened the door, stepping out only seconds before Van caught me up in his arms in a crushing hug. "Are you okay?" he asked against my hair.

You know, it was kind of nice to be held and worried about. I mean, if I wasn't worried about cracked ribs and all. But, for a moment, I felt safe and secure, real secure, and loved.

"I'm fine," I gasped, trying to delicately loosen his hold. "Really, Van, I'm fine."

This man was not easily deterred.

"I'm fine," I choked out, finding it even harder to breathe. "But I can't breathe."

"Why can't you breathe?" He exclaimed, immediately loosening his hold, so he could look at me.

"Because you were hugging the stuffing out of her," Kyle said casually, as he walked past us. "Best get her in the house and fed before Franklin shows up."

"Why? Why would Franklin be showing up?" Van asked, turning toward Kyle.

Momma appeared next to Kyle. "Because L.J. here not only saved the lives of all of the people in the bank," Momma inserted. "But also talked both armed bank robbers into putting their guns down and surrendering."

I glared at her.

She gasped softly. "But I wasn't supposed to say that, was I?" she said apologetically.

"No, you were not," I replied.

"What?" Van exclaimed and turned back to me. "What did you do?"

"Why don't we all go inside," Kyle suggested. "L.J. can put her feet up and I can get these leftovers into the house before they completely go bad."

That's right! I'd almost forgotten about the extra desserts.

"Fine," Van agreed. "And Bea sent over a picnic basket for dinner. Said she figured you'd be about wiped out after the weekend you'd had. Fried chicken and all the fixings."

I know I'd said I wasn't hungry about an hour ago, but all the excitement must have given me an appetite because I was starving. "Bless Bea," I replied. "Let's go in and eat!"

"Y'all go in," Van said, taking hold of my hand. "I just want a minute with L.J."

Kyle and Momma went into the house, Kyle grabbing the picnic basket that was laying on the front porch as he went by it and then closing the door behind him.

Van gently turned me towards him and tenderly stroked my cheek. "Are you okay?" he asked, searching my eyes. "You've been through so much lately. I just can't imagine..."

Now this, this was sugar. Having this big, strong man worrying and caring about me. I couldn't stop myself, I leaned up, slipped my arms around his neck, and pressed my lips against his. "I am now," I whispered.

And as he wrapped his arms around me and deepened the kiss, I knew there was nothing better than how I was feeling at this moment in time.

Chapter Twelve

"I called Bud," Kyle said when I got downstairs after changing out of my work clothes. "He's going to head down to the jail straight away."

They were all sitting at the kitchen table, unpacking Bea's generous picnic basket.

"Good Old Bud," I said as I slipped into my chair.

Kyle grinned, as he poured himself a tall glass of sweet tea. "And you wanna know the crazy thing?"

"What?" I asked.

"When I told him that you would be able to show him where their grammy hid her money in order to pay for his fees, he didn't seem to question it at all," he replied.

"Some people are accepting of things they don't quite understand," Momma said. "Bud was one to always keep an open mind."

"Unlike a certain Mississippi Bureau of Investigations agent," Kyle added as he chose a piece of chicken from the plate at the center of the table.

66

"Can you please explain to me why Franklin wants to interview you?" Van asked as he passed the bowl of potato salad in my direction.

I shrugged, as I scooped a little bit of the salad onto my plate. "I guess he overheard me telling the bank robbers about their grandma," I said.

"So? However you were able to talk those men down and get them to surrender their weapons has no bearing on the case," Van said.

"There's a couple of things that aren't sitting right with me," Kyle said, pointing a chicken leg as he spoke.

"Such as?" Momma asked.

But before Kyle could answer, the doorbell rang.

"It's probably Franklin," I sighed, and I pushed my chair away from the table.

"No, honey, you just sit tight," Momma insisted. "I'll get the door."

"But Momma…"

She smiled at me. "Maybe it's time for Franklin to learn to have an open mind."

67

She glided out of the room with a chuckle.

"I don't like this," I said anxiously. "I don't have a good feeling about this at all."

Van leaned back in his chair and smiled. "Oh, I don't know," he said. "I think your momma has the right idea. Might show us who we're dealing with."

"And what happens if…" I lowered my voice. "The Sons of Mississippi find out that I'm talking with my momma?"

Both Van and Kyle looked alarmed at the same time. See, that's what you get when you're so wrapped up in male ego, that you don't think about the consequences.

Well, we better do some pretty fast thinking now.

I could hear the door open.

"Hello," Franklin called from the hallway.

"We're all back here, in the kitchen," I shouted back.

I heard his footsteps on the floor coming towards us, then I heard the door close behind him and the footsteps stopped. Then I heard the click of the deadbolt locking and suddenly the footsteps hurried in our direction.

"Damn," I whispered.

Kyle bit back a smile.

"Not funny," I whispered harshly.

Franklin walked into the kitchen, looking a little perplexed.

"Your front door opened by itself," he blurted out.

I shrugged. "It's an old drafty house," I replied. "It happens."

"But then it closed itself and locked the deadbolt," he added.

"Right?" Van inserted. "Works pretty slick, doesn't it?"

Franklin turned to Van. "What?" he asked.

"The new automatic lock," he said. "I just put it in, and we've been testing it out. Just another safety precaution I wanted L.J. to have."

Well, bless his heart, that was downright brilliant.

"Have a seat," I offered to Franklin. "We were just starting dinner."

"Thank you," he said. "If you don't mind."

"Heaven's no," Kyle replied, getting up and pulling an extra plate and silverware out for Franklin. "We have more than enough."

He placed them in front of Franklin, poured him a sweet tea, and then sat down. "So, how can we help you?" Kyle asked.

Franklin abruptly turned away from Kyle and faced me. "How did you know about their grandmother?" he asked.

Chapter Thirteen

"Grammy Anderson?" I replied, as casually as I could while I secretly wiped my sweaty palms on my jeans underneath the table. "Well, Momma let me know she passed when I was living in New York."

Then I smiled broadly. "Why? Do you actually think I have some secret psychic powers that I'm not telling you about?" I asked. "Like I have a psychic hotline number on the side?"

Franklin looked a little embarrassed and I felt a huge wave of relief. Maybe he was going to actually believe me.

"Course not," he said. "But you seemed...convincing."

"I sure hope so," I replied. "I was scared to death, though. The younger one seemed so nervous with that gun. I thought for sure he was going to accidentally shoot someone."

I glanced over at Kyle and saw that he was frantically texting someone.

Really? I could use a little support here.

"So, how did you know?" Franklin asked.

"How did I know what?" I asked, confused.

"That they were the Anderson boys?" he replied. And now, he didn't look embarrassed at all. He looked like he just caught his rabbit in the trap. "Weren't they wearing masks? How did you know it was them?"

Dang!

"Cause LeRoy called Jasper by name when they came in the bank door," Kyle said, sliding his phone face down onto the table. "I'm guessing there ain't too many Jaspers round town."

"I don't remember that," Franklin said.

"Well, it happened when they first walked in the bank," Kyle said. "So, maybe you weren't there yet."

"We were…" Franklin began to say, then he stopped.

This time he didn't look embarrassed, he looked panicked.

There was a moment of uncomfortable silence. I mean, what do you do when a Mississippi Bureau of Investigations agent nearly admits to being at the bank before the robbery actually happens?

I voted for letting him off the hook. For now.

"Well, I'm sure it will be on the bank's video recording," I blurted out, and then I smiled at Franklin. "Right? All the banks have those cameras to record things like that."

He nodded. "Er, right," he agreed cautiously. "They all do."

I shrugged happily and took a sip of my drink. "Well, great, that's solved," I said. "So, do you want some supper?"

"No. No, thank you," he said shortly, pushing his chair away from the table. "I've got more work to do tonight."

"Are you sure?" I asked. "I would make up a plate and send it with you."

He smiled, and it actually did reach his eyes. "Thank you, Louella Jo," he said. "I've got to say that you sounded just like your momma when you said that. She was always trying to feed me."

My eyes moistened slightly, and I smiled back at him. "Thank you," I said, adding a little hoarseness to my voice, just for effect. "That's actually a very sweet thing to hear. I'm glad you have good memories of her."

"I do," he said, reaching over and taking my hands in his.

I am so glad I wiped my sweaty palms on my jeans.

"I have wonderful memories of both your momma and you," he said, searching my eyes. "Wonderful memories."

"So, is the bank going to press charges?" Van asked loudly.

Franklin dropped my hands, stood up, and turned to Van. "I believe they are," he replied. "After all, it was an attempted robbery."

Van stood up too. "But they put down their weapons and gave up on their own accord."

I sighed, leaned back in my chair, picked up my chicken leg, and took a bite.

"Well, we'll just have to see what the judge decides," Franklin said curtly.

He glanced at me and nodded. "I'll be in touch," he said to me.

"We'll look forward to it," Van replied.

"Thank you," I said. "Let me show you out."

He shook his head. "No need," he said. "Besides, I want to see what that fancy door of yours does when someone is leaving."

Momma winked at me, then hurried down the hallway.

"I sure hope you're impressed," I said.

And I sure hope you're fooled, I thought.

He turned and headed down the hall. I heard the deadbolts unlock and the door open before his footsteps hit the front hallway.

"How are we going to explain…" I began.

Van hurried over to the kitchen door. "I hit the controls for you," he shouted. "I haven't added an inside sensor yet. Y'all have a good night."

The door closed, Momma locked the deadbolt and I about collapsed in my chair.

Chapter Fourteen

"That was…" Kyle began before I frantically shook my head to shut him up.

"What?" he asked.

I got up, walked over to the blender on the counter, and turned it on. "Do we have to worry about bugs?" I asked.

"What?" Kyle and Van shouted.

"Do we have to worry about bugs?" I asked, raising my voice a mite.

"What?" they both replied.

"Do we have to…." I began to shout. Then Momma turned off the blender. So, the words, "WORRY ABOUT BUGS?" echoed throughout the whole house and maybe even the neighborhood.

Van grinned, picked up the flyswatter hanging on the wall, and slapped it, loudly, against the counter.

"Nope," he yelled back. "Looks like I got it."

I leaned back against the counter and shook my head. "I have no idea why I am not already in jail," I said softly.

Van came over and kissed my forehead. "Obviously because you have such brilliant partners working with you," he teased.

"Hey, listen, some of us were brilliant," Kyle replied. "Who do you think was frantically texting Bud for the names of his new clients while Franklin was slowly leading you down the garden path?"

"That was brilliant," I agreed. "And I walked right into that one. I thought I had him flustered."

Van put his arm around my shoulders and guided me back to the table. Then he bent down and checked under the table near where Franklin had been sitting.

"No bugs," he said, then he took his seat. "You did have him flustered. But he's good. And smart."

"What's interesting is his little slip-up," Kyle said. "He was already at the bank when the bank robbers walked in. I did think their arrival was both timely and discreet, too discreet."

"So, were they given a tip about the robbery?" I asked. "It almost seems like a set-up."

"Probably was a set-up," Momma said, taking her seat at the table. "I betcha the state of Mississippi is itching to get its hands on Grammy Anderson's files."

"What? Why?" I asked.

Momma sat back and smiled widely. "Y'all know that Mississippi didn't repeal statewide Prohibition laws until 1966, right?"

"What?" Kyle asked. "Mississippi was a dry state until then?"

"Well, local governments held elections, so the residents could decide if they wanted to allow liquor in their county or not," Momma explained. "But we are in one of the counties that wanted to stay dry."

"I didn't know that," Van said.

"Well, honey, it was a little before your time," Momma explained. "And there was a law on the books that said that if any Mississippi politician was found drunk, or in a state of intoxication from the use of liquor, they would be charged with a high misdemeanor and removed from office."

She paused for a moment. "You know, I don't know if that law was ever repealed," she mused. "Anyway, Grammy Anderson was something of an entrepreneur in these parts. She ran one of the best diners in the area. Everyone loved Grammy Anderson's biscuits and gravy or fried catfish and cheesy grits. But what most folks don't know, is that back behind the diner, down some steps and through a thick oak door, Grammy ran the finest little speakeasy in the area."

"A speakeasy?" Kyle exclaimed. "You mean like mobsters and molls, bathtub gin, and white lightning?"

Momma laughed and shook her head. "No, it wasn't like the prohibition era when it was hard to buy good liquor. Grammy's was a fashionable establishment. Leather seats, roomy booths, hardwood floors, soft lighting, and brass fittings on the bar," she grinned at me.

"Not that I would know. But I heard my parents talk about it when I was younger."

"Grandma and Grandpa Buchanan went to a speakeasy?" I exclaimed, remembering those two church-going, Bible-thumping, well-respected citizens of Julep.

"Only on special occasions," Momma laughed. "And, like most of the other clients, only because they knew that Grammy was very discreet."

"But discreet doesn't mean naïve," Van inserted.

Momma looked up at him and nodded. "Exactly," she said. "Word is, Grammy kept files on all of her customers. Files that helped everyone play nice."

"But no one today would care if people went to bars back then," I said. "So, what's the big deal about Grammy's files?"

"Well, I heard those notes weren't just about drinking," Momma said. "Grammy was a smart woman who listened more than she talked and remembered what people said. Especially people whose lips were loose with liquor." Then Momma slowly looked at each one of us.

"Especially men who were part of an organization called The Sons of Mississippi."

Chapter Fifteen

I put my elbows on the table, (something I normally would not have gotten away with doing) cradled my head in my hands, and tried to make sense of everything that was going on.

"Okay," I said, as I stared down at the kitchen table and tried to gather my thoughts. "Can I just say that if I never hear the words 'Sons of Mississippi' again, I will die a happy woman."

I looked up and saw the concerned looks on the faces across the table from me.

"Come on," I sighed. "I'm not going over the edge, but can I just take a minute and list all of the places that those damn Sons of Mississippi have intersected in my life during the past few months?"

I could feel Momma's cold touch on my shoulder. "You go right ahead, sweetie," she soothed.

Yep, she thought I was going over the edge.

I took a deep breath and then started. "Okay, JoEllen meets Ridge at a Sons of Mississippi event where she's waitressing. Ridge and JoEllen start dating, but his daddy doesn't like it, so he lies to Ridge about JoEllen seeing someone else. Ridge beats JoEllen about to death. And daddy doesn't want to be bothered with bringing her to a hospital and all the fuss that would entail, so they drop her body into the Gulf."

"Right," Van said, slowly nodding his head in agreement. "And when JoEllen is nearly dead, she hears some girls asking for help."

I nod slowly. "Which is why she can't rest, because those girls want help."

"And those girls, are they in the same situation as Amanda Lee?" Kyle asked.

"I really hope that Amanda Lee is not in that situation," I said. "But I'm afraid she might be."

"So, how do we help Amanda Lee?" Kyle asked. "And how do we help those girls? And how do we get JoEllen to be at peace?"

I held up my hand to stop him and then took a deep breath. "Okay, give me a minute," I said. "I don't want to get ahead of myself. I just need to do this in chronological order, so I don't forget anything."

"You're right. Chronological is good. You just take your time," Kyle agreed. "And we can help fill in any blanks."

"Okay, so next, they come looking for Momma because they think JoEllen told her something," I said. "We think they send Deputy Hill to kill Momma."

"And they still don't have the card file," Kyle added.

"That's right," I replied, a little confused. "After all that trouble, why aren't they still trying to get it."

"Because you don't have it," Van said. "It was mailed back to you from New York."

"That's right," I said. "They've got someone watching for it at the post office."

"Okay, so next you get the middle-of-the-night phone call about the rendezvous on the beach," Kyle said.

85

I nodded. "And then someone shoots Deputy Hill," I said, then I turned and smiled at Van. "And Van gets his first chance to save my life, not realizing that he's going to have a whole bunch of opportunities after that one."

"Lots of opportunities," he teased, returning my smile.

"So, after that Mr. Murphy from the bank tries to intimidate me into selling him the salon," I continued. "And when I was in his office, I had a real bad feeling about something in his files."

"And then you call Bud in to help you and changed my life," Kyle said.

"Yes, I did, and don't you forget it."

"Then you took the waitressing job, got accosted by Tucker, saved by Sheriff King, and finally, got to meet Ridge Patterson and his dad," Van said. "That was a busy night for you."

"And I also found out that Mayor Newsom was involved somehow," I said. "And I met Shelby Adair, who is also involved somehow."

"This cast of characters is getting out of hand," Momma said.

"Right?" I agreed. "So, then we have Ridge trying to kill me. Sheriff King saving my life. Sheriff King murdered, but not before he worked with Shelby to make Ridge's death look like a suicide."

"Amanda Lee goes missing right about then too," Kyle inserted.

I nodded. "Right. And just when we're figuring that out, Franklin comes to town to investigate Sheriff King's murder and Deputy Hill's disappearance."

"We go to Ridge's funeral and find a creepy secret room in the mansion," Van said.

"You did what?" Kyle asked.

"You went home to clean," I reminded him. "And then I came home and had that vision about Van, so I went to the Crenshaw Place by myself."

"Wait, we went to the Crenshaw Place before that," Van said. "That's where we found Hill's body."

That's right!

I nodded at him. "That's why I needed to do this," I said. "Everything is running together. And I just have to talk it out, to make sure I'm not missing something important."

Kyle got up and walked over to the kitchen counter, opened a drawer, and pulled out an old composition notebook from the drawer.

"What in the world?" I asked.

"I found it when I was searching for a corkscrew," he said. "By the way, you don't have a corkscrew."

"It's in the dining room," Momma inserted. "In the candle drawer."

We all turned and looked at Momma.

"Okay, I'll ask," I volunteered. "Why in the world is the corkscrew in the candle drawer?"

"Because it's just perfect to get the candle stubs out of the candle holders," she said. "Slips right in and grabs 'em. Easy peasy."

Kyle shrugged and walked back to his chair. "Can't argue with that kind of logic," he said, opening the notebook. "Now, give me a second to write down everything we've talked about so far, and then you can continue."

Chapter Sixteen

"Okay, I have it all down," Kyle said, a few minutes later.

"How did you get it all down so quickly?" I asked, amazed.

He held up the notebook to display characters that seem to be a cross between ancient Egyptian hieroglyphics and chicken scratch.

"What the hell is that?" I asked.

"Shorthand," Kyle replied, looking offended. "I took it in high school."

"Did you go to high school in ancient Egypt?" I asked.

"It's not that bad," he said, handing the notebook to Van. "Right?"

Van looked at the page, then turned it upside down, then back right side up. "It's pretty bad," he said. "And I worked in the cryptanalysis area of the bureau for a couple of months." He studied it again. "Yep, I got nothing."

"Fine," Kyle sighed. "I'll get it typed up and send it to all of you." He turned to Momma. "Do you want me to print it out for you?"

She smiled at him and shook her head. "No, sweetie, I can read it just fine," she replied, then she winked at him. "Course, I was an archeology major in college."

"Everyone's a comedienne," Kyle moaned.

"Well, the only thing you have to add is this past weekend," I said. "Two funerals, two trips to the Crenshaw house, one vision, finding the portfolio, encountering a demon, and Myrtle's death."

I sat back in my chair and shook my head. "Well, it's no wonder I'm worn slap out, y'all," I said. "All of this happened since I've been home, and we haven't even really started investigating them."

"Have you looked through the portfolio?" Kyle asked as he jotted down the rest of the information.

"No," I confessed. "I was so wrapped up with Myrtle's death and all, I about forgot that I had it. We could look at it now."

"I think there's something else we should do first," Van said.

"What's that?" I asked, wondering what could be more important than those names.

"I've been thinking about Franklin's little slip-up, about being there before the robbery occurred," Van said. "And it's just not sitting right with me. I agree with your momma, there's stuff at the old speakeasy that could be damaging to the Sons of Mississippi. It would be interesting to discover how those two young men decided on robbing the bank."

Kyle nodded. "Interesting to see if someone suggested it to them."

Van smiled. "Right. Did they get a little nudge in the wrong direction?"

"So, you're thinking someone wanted them out of the way, so they could search Grammy's place?" I asked, feeling once again like I was either in the middle of a Twilight Zone episode, or some crime show based in the deep South.

"Well, Grammy told you herself, somewhere in there, there's a whole lot of money hidden away," Kyle added, then he looked at Van. "What do you think we should do next?"

"I think you ought to text Bud and see if we can get the boys' permission to enter the speakeasy and look for the cash," he began, then turned to me and winked, "and if we happen to find anything else interesting when we're searching, so much the better."

"Good idea," I agreed. "Really good idea."

"Texting right now," Kyle said, as his fingers flew across the phone's keyboard. A moment later he looked up. "Bud says they're fine with us looking, seeing as Grammy talked to L.J., and not them. But Bud would like to come along, make sure this is all legal-like."

"That's smart," I said. "In case some troopers suddenly show up, it would be nice to have a lawyer with us."

Kyle texted our response back, then nodded. "He said he can meet us there in twenty minutes," he said.

"That gives us about five minutes to change and get going," I said.

"Wait? What? Five minutes?" Kyle exclaimed. "Girl, I can't get ready in five minutes."

I smiled at Kyle. "Oh, don't worry, sweetie," I teased. "It'll be dark. Bud probably won't even notice."

He stared at me for a long moment, his lips pursed and his face solemn. "That was harsh, L.J," he finally said and then he winked. "Challenge accepted."

Four and a half minutes later, I hurried down the stairs in my choice of appropriate dress for searching an old speakeasy at night - black jeans, a black t-shirt, and dark running shoes. Kyle met me at the base of the staircase in his idea of appropriate dress – a bright red floral, short-sleeved silk camp shirt, a pair of white linen pants, white loafers, and a straw Panama hat on his head.

"Dang, challenge accepted, and challenge accomplished. You look amazing," I said, totally in awe of his fashion sense and speed.

Kyle grinned widely, then patted his hand against his chest. "I dressed so quickly, I nearly perspired," he teased.

"In the South, we call that glowing," I explained.

Kyle laughed. "Whatever you call it, you don't want it anywhere near silk," he replied.

"And you're wearing it to search an old, abandoned building?" Van asked, totally confused.

"No, I'm wearing it to impress Bud," Kyle replied. "Searching the building is just the backdrop."

"Well, we have fourteen minutes to get to that backdrop," I reminded everyone. "So, we'd better leave now."

Chapter Seventeen

"Why didn't you wear a red silk shirt and fancy trousers for me?" Van asked as we drove toward the speakeasy.

"Because you would have thought I was nuts," I replied evenly.

He chuckled softly. "You're right," he said, then he glanced over at me before turning back to pay attention to the road. "Although, there is something sexy about a woman dressed in all black too."

"Really?" I asked, as a warm flutter developed in my midsection. "Sexy, huh?"

"Very sexy," he replied softly.

"All right, all right," Kyle complained from the back seat. "Stop flirting and concentrate on getting to the speakeasy as quickly as possible, okay?"

There was none of the usual humor in Kyle's voice, instead, there was tension and fear.

"Why? What's wrong?" I asked, turning in my seat to look at Kyle.

He took a deep breath, and I could see that he was debating whether or not he should tell me. Then, it seemed that his internal argument was over with a nod of his head. "I just got a text from Bud," he admitted. "He thinks someone might be following him. But he didn't want to worry anyone."

"Well, you're worried, right?" I asked.

"Yeah. Yes, I am," he confessed.

"Do you know where he is?" Van asked.

"Yeah, I've been following him on my phone," he said. "He just off the main highway, about five miles out of town."

"That's not too far from Myrtle's place," I said. "Why don't you call him and have him meet us there?"

"That's a good idea," Van agreed. "The entrance to Myrtle's place is just beyond a bend and is pretty well hidden. He should be able to almost disappear right in front of them."

"And what if they follow him?" Kyle asked, not sounding too excited about the plan.

"Well, he was Myrtle's lawyer, so he could tell them he was working on her estate," I suggested. "Besides, there's something about Myrtle's place that watches over folk. I really think he'd be safe there."

"Okay, I'll call him," Kyle said.

"Let him know we're only about five or so minutes down the road from him," Van added. "So, in case they follow him, he won't have to sweet talk them for too long."

While Kyle talked to Bud, Van turned to me, his eyes filled with concern.

"What?" I asked immediately. "You don't think Myrtle's is a good idea?"

"No, it's a good plan," he said, keeping his voice low. "But what bothers me is the fact that Bud knew they were following him. They didn't even try to hide themselves."

"So, are they stupid, cocky, or do they know the cards are stacked in their favor, so they don't have to worry?" I whispered back.

He nodded slowly. "Right," he said. "I wish I knew the answer to those questions. I'm really hoping stupid – but stupid people can be even more dangerous than cocky ones."

"How much faster can we go without getting a ticket?" I asked.

Van glanced in the rearview mirror and then quickly back in my direction. "Not any faster than I'm going now," he said, his jaw tense. "Looks like we've got ourselves a tail too."

I looked in the side mirror and saw the police cruiser following us. "Looks like Franklin's vehicle," I said with a sigh. "I really wanted to believe that he was on the side of the good guys."

Van sent me a searching look, then turned back to the road. "Why?" he finally asked.

"Why what?" I replied.

"Why did you want Franklin to be a good guy?"

I shrugged. "Well, he was my best friend all through high school," I explained. "We helped each other through some hard times, and I always used to be able to trust him. It's just sad, you know. Another part of my childhood gone. People you thought you could always rely on, changing. And not for the better."

He nodded slowly, then exhaled. "I need to confess," he said. "I was a little worried that you were still interested in him."

"Interested?" I asked. "As in…dating interested?"

"Yeah," he said, with a note of embarrassment. "Like that."

"Well, I might have been if I hadn't met you first," I said, surprised at my audacity. "But I have no feelings like that for him. He's just an old friend."

"I'm relieved to hear you say that," Van said with a smile. "Really relieved."

I was a little surprised at the satisfaction his words gave me. I mean, I would never purposely try and make

100

someone feel jealous, but it was a kind of heady feeling to know that Van was concerned that other men would find me attractive.

Hmmm, L.J. Carter, femme fatale.

Yeah, more like L.J. Carter, babe in the woods.

And speaking of woods...

"There's the entrance to Myrtle's place," I said as I pointed ahead to the narrow path. "Let's hope Bud is the only one there."

Chapter Eighteen

We pulled down the long narrow lane, branches brushing either side of Van's truck as we drove down it. The sun was nearly totally blocked by the overgrowth. and it was like traveling through a tunnel...

...to another world.

That thought came unbidden to my mind, but I felt the truth of it as soon as I stepped out of the car. The air around us was thick with otherworldly energy and I wondered if anyone else could feel it. The scents of the vegetation were heavy in the humid air. A chorus of frogs, crickets, and night birds surrounded us in all directions. The sun was low in the sky, but we still had another hour or so of light.

Van held back the branches that blocked the path and I moved forward to the clearing, hoping that we would only find Bud's truck parked ahead.

"Are we in the shire?" Kyle asked, stepping gingerly around the silk-snagging brush. "Or...what's the name of the fairy kingdom?"

"Rivendell," Van and I replied together, then laughed softly.

"And they were elves," Van added.

"Whatever," Kyle said. "This is just like that place."

"Yes, it is," Bud agreed, stepping around a large oak tree into the path. "In more ways than we will ever realize."

"Are you okay?" Kyle asked, concern thick in his voice.

Bud smiled tenderly at Kyle and nodded. "Yeah, but thanks for being worried."

Kyle shrugged. "I just...you know... wanted..."

Then we heard another vehicle driving up the narrow lane and Kyle stopped talking to gaze behind us.

I turned to Van. "Looks like we've got company," I said.

103

He nodded. "Your old friend doesn't like taking 'no' for an answer."

"Old friend?" Bud asked.

"Franklin Abney," I said.

"Wait. That MBI agent is chubby Frankie?" Bud asked, shaking his head.

"I hope you never called him that to his face," Kyle said.

Bud shook his head. "No, of course not," he replied. "Matter of fact, I represented his folks. I was the executor for their estate."

"They died?" I asked, shocked. "His parents died?"

"He didn't tell you?" Bud asked.

I shook my head. "I didn't...I feel so bad, going on about my momma..."

"Hey, no need for that," Bud said. "You had no idea, and you are entitled to your own feelings and your own grief."

Yeah, I was. But maybe I just needed to be a little nicer to Franklin in the future. He'd been through a lot more than I knew.

I could hear the muffled steps of regulation shoes against the soft ground as Franklin got closer. We all just stood around the path and watched as he made his way around Van's truck.

"Hey, Franklin," I said, feeling a little more empathy for him. "Did you need something more?"

He looked around at all of us and seemed a little uncomfortable. "I was just wondering…I mean, I thought you were tired…I mean…"

"I called Louella Jo to see if she had some time to meet me at Myrtle's," Bud said, stepping in to save the day.

"Why?" Franklin asked.

"Is there some law against folks meeting past eight o'clock at night in Mississippi?" Kyle asked.

"No. No, of course not," Franklin stammered. "But since Louella Jo has been involved in so many…"

105

"Louella Jo is Myrtle's beneficiary," Bud interrupted.

My first thought was —Dang it, Bud, I wanted Franklin to finish that sentence.

My second thought was— What the hell?

I turned to Bud and was about to question him, but thankfully the look in his eyes warned me to wait on any questions I might have until later.

Instead, I pulled a tissue out of my pocket and dabbed my eyes. "I still can't believe it," I whispered. "I can't believe she's gone."

Franklin looked even more uneasy. "Oh, I didn't realize," he said. "I didn't..." Then he paused, looked at Van and Kyle and his eyes narrowed. "And why are you both here?"

Van met Franklin's eyes, took a step closer to me, and deliberately slipped his arm around my shoulders.

"I have a vested interest in L.J.'s safety," Van replied easily. "A very personal vested interest."

Whether he was warning Franklin off or letting him know that he was watching over me, I'm not sure. I'm guessing it was a little of both. But it worked, Franklin's eyes hardened, and he nodded curtly. "Well, thank you for your time, folks," he said, then abruptly turned and strode back down the lane.

"I think we might have hurt his feelings," I said, regretting the look in his eyes.

Bud slowly shook his head. "Yeah, maybe," he said, looking down the lane. "Or it might just be that Franklin is trolling the waters right now until he can reel us in."

I waited until we heard Franklin's vehicle drive away before I said anything else. Then I turned to Bud and asked the question that had been troubling me. "Did Myrtle really leave me her house?" I asked with obvious concern on my face.

He smiled down at me. "Don't get all worked up, sweetie. She left it to the entire book club," he said. "So, I guess technically that means you too, doesn't it?"

I felt a wave of relief wash over me. I was practically a stranger to Myrtle, even though she was my new spirit guide, and I certainly did not feel that I deserved to be left anything.

"That's great," I said. "I'm glad she did that. This place needs to be watched over by people who understand it."

He nodded. "I agree, and that's what Myrtle wanted," he said. "But now, I think we all ought to head over to the speakeasy and see if we can't find something to help my clients."

He turned to Kyle. "Want to drive with me?"

I saw happiness brighten Kyle's face at the request.

"Yeah, that would be great," he agreed.

Bud nodded and started toward the truck. Finally, just before they climbed in, I overheard Bud whisper, "Nice outfit."

"Oh, this old thing," Kyle replied with a shrug as he opened the door. "Why, I only wear it when I don't care how I look."

Bud laughed and met Kyle's eyes over the bed of the truck. "It's A Wonderful Life, right?"

"You know your old movies. Got it on one," Kyle replied with a responding chuckle.

They climbed into Bud's truck, ending my eavesdropping, and I sighed softly.

"You okay?" Van asked.

"Yeah," I said with a nod. "I just love seeing Kyle this happy."

He tightened his arm around my shoulders and gave me a quick squeeze. "You are a good friend," he said, placing a quick kiss on my forehead. "Now, let's go check out a speakeasy."

Chapter Nineteen

Do you know what's scarier than an abandoned building that's overgrown with kudzu, with boarded-up doors and windows peeking through the dense vegetation, a half-demolished brick chimney, rotted out porch stairs, and a strange animal making scampering sounds at your feet as you walk down the narrow path as the sun sets behind you?

That's right. Absolutely nothing!

"This was a classy speakeasy?" I whispered incredulously as we neared the front door.

"Why are you whispering?" Van asked.

I froze in my steps and thought about it for a moment. "I have no idea," I replied. "Maybe so the ghosts don't hear us?"

Bud and Kyle had already – miraculously – made it up the steps and Bud was unlocking the padlock on the front door. "Hey, the boys said it looks a lot worse from the outside," he called to us. "The inside should be fine."

"Well, honestly, it couldn't be any worse than the outside," I said as I stepped gingerly onto the first step. Then I shook my head, remembering the Crenshaw Mansion. "Forget I said that. It could be worse. It could be a lot worse."

Bud uncoupled the lock from the door and laid it on the seat of a ramshackle porch swing hanging by only one chain next to the door. He pushed the door open, leaned in, and flipped on the light switch.

"There's electricity in there?" I asked, amazed.

"Yep, and running water," Bud said, entering the house. "The boys said that they got a little lazy with the landscaping during the past year."

Kyle shuddered. "How fast does that stuff out there grow?"

"Kudzu," Bud explained. "The vine that just about ate the south. It grows about a foot a day."

"Are you kidding me?" Kyle asked, astonished.

"Wait," I exclaimed. "You grew up in Baton Rouge, right? How come you don't know kudzu?"

"Honey, I grew up in the inner city. The only green I saw around the apartments we lived in was some scraggly, brown excuse for grass separating the concrete sidewalks from the concrete parking lot from the concrete buildings," he replied.

"Well, just so you know, you stand still outside long enough and you're a goner," Van teased.

Kyle looked at Van, then looked at the creeping plant at the exact moment the vine shook because of a slight breeze. Van grinned. "Looks like it's coming to get you," he warned. "I understand they like silk shirts."

Kyle shuddered and quickly followed Bud into the house. "I am so out of here," he said.

Laughing, Van and I followed him but paused in surprise when we saw the inside of the house.

Kyle stood next to us, his hands on his hips, shaking his head as he looked over the collection of garbage and debris scattered all over the room. From decaying used pizza boxes to enough beer cans to make a recycler a small fortune, the room was like a disgusting dorm room on steroids.

"This was the speakeasy?" I asked, astonished.

Bud shook his head. "No, this was their house, on the same property as the diner and the speakeasy," he explained. "We have to drive a couple hundred yards further up the road to get to those buildings. And if you think the kudzu is bad here, wait until you see the diner."

"I think I'll take my chances with the people-eating plants," Kyle said, waving his hand in front of his face. "This place is disgusting."

"I know it is!"

I jumped when Grammy Anderson appeared next to me, mirroring the same stance Kyle had taken. "Those boys are getting on my last nerve," she exclaimed. "They weren't raised in a barn, much less a pig stye. Why are they all acting like they were?"

"Maybe it's their way of grieving," I replied.

"Who are you talking to?" Kyle asked.

I glanced around to see all three men staring at me with concern on their faces.

"Oh, sorry," I quickly stammered. "Grammy is here, and she was just remarking on the state of this room."

"I wasn't remarking," Grammy inserted. "I am fit to be tied. Those boys were raised better than this."

"She said that the boys know better than this," I explained. "And she is fit to be tied."

"I don't blame her one little bit," Kyle replied. "There is no excuse for this."

Grammy turned and smiled at Kyle. "Oh, I like that pretty man," she said. "He's got a good head on his shoulders."

I laughed and nodded at her.

"What did she say?" Kyle asked.

Grinning, I explained. "She said that you have a good head on your shoulders and that you were a pretty man."

Kyle smiled widely. "Damn straight!" he agreed.

Bud turned to me and winked. "Highly improbable," he said sardonically.

Chapter Twenty

Before Kyle could reply to Bud's remark a thunderous pounding on the door interrupted our conversation.

"At this hour," Grammy scolded. "Ain't no one got any manners these days."

"Let me answer it," Bud said, moving his six-and-a-half-foot frame quickly across the room to the door behind me.

He positioned himself so he blocked the view of the room with his body and opened the door a crack. "May I help you?" he asked.

"I'm here to arrest you for breaking and entering," Franklin's voice wafted through the doorway.

Bud chuckled softly and nodded slowly. "Are you now?" he asked with humor. Then he stepped to the side. "Well, you may as well come in while you read me my rights."

Franklin pushed into the house and froze, looking slowly at the rest of us in the room. "What the hell are y'all doing here?" he demanded.

Bud closed the door and then casually turned to Franklin. "Well, as you know, I am the legal representative for LeRoy and Jasper Anderson," Bud explained easily. "And, as they gave me the key to their house with specific instructions to enter and it and locate some things for them, I'm afraid you won't be arresting anyone tonight."

"Do you have proof?" Franklin asked belligerently.

"Do I have your permission to reach into my jacket for an envelope?" he asked politely, as opposite in his demeanor from Franklin as night from day.

"Yes. Go ahead," Franklin snapped.

Bud pulled out an ivory-colored envelope with the logo of his law office embossed on the corner in gold. Then he opened the envelope, pulled out a piece of matching stationery, and handed it to Franklin. "As you

117

can see," he patiently explained. "My clients have given me permission to go through the premises to search for anything that might in any way aid in their defense. In other words, I have carte blanche to explore their property."

I could see the frustration in Franklin's eyes and, once again, I felt sorry for him. It seemed like he was being thwarted at every turn.

He handed the paper back to Bud and then turned to us. "And how about them?" he asked. "Why are they here? I don't see their names on your document."

Bud leaned against the wall and nodded. "First, legally, you'll note that the document names me, Bud Featherstone, and then additionally names any agents I might deem necessary in the execution of my duties," he said. "These folks here are my agents."

"And why do you need agents?" Franklin asked skeptically.

Bud smiled sheepishly. "Well, to tell you the truth, I could pretty much have done this whole search by my lonesome," he said with a shrug. "I mean, really, there's not much space in this place."

"So?" Franklin prompted.

"Well, with all that talk about ghosts and such, I gotta admit, I kinda got the heebie-jeebies and I sure didn't like the idea of coming out here all by my lonesome, late at night," he admitted. "So, since we were all at Myrtle's place anyhow, I asked them to come on along. Seems a mite less scary when you have company."

Franklin shook his head and looked slowly at each of us. "So, you want me to believe that you were afraid of the dark and needed the rest of the Scooby Team to come along with you while you searched your client's house?"

Bud nodded. "Pretty much," he replied.

"I have a hard time believing that an educated man like you would be frightened by a ghost story about a dead old lady," he scoffed.

"Well, that young man is nothing but rude," Grammy huffed and before I could stop her, she kicked a pile of empty beer cans, sending them crashing across the floor.

"What the hell was that?" Franklin exclaimed, jumping and turning toward the sound.

"I believe that would be your ghost story," Bud replied easily.

"And she would have gotten away with it if those meddling kids hadn't shown up," Kyle whispered to me.

I snorted out loud, then quickly slapped my hands over my mouth.

Franklin looked at me and I could see the disappointment in his eyes. Then he turned to Bud. "I have a source who believes that this property might also hold evidence from another crime," he said. "I'd like to search the property with you."

Bud nodded slowly. "Sure, as soon as you bring me a warrant."

"I assure you, my source is a highly respected individual," Franklin replied.

"Makes no matter to me who he is," Bud said. "The law is the law, which is what makes this country great. You bring me a warrant; I'll be happy to come on out here with you and search."

"I'll have the congressman sign it himself," Franklin said, and I gasped softly in surprise.

Bud shot a quick look at me, then turned back to Franklin. "Well, you go ahead and have that congressman sign in, but if it doesn't also have the signature of the county judge on it too, it ain't worth the paper it's printed on."

"But he's a congressman," Franklin argued.

"But the law doesn't give him any jurisdiction on search warrants," Bud said. "But seeing how important he is, I'm sure he's fishing buddies with one of the judges, so it shouldn't be all that hard to get that warrant."

Bud pushed himself off the wall and walked over to the door, opening it widely. "I'll be in my office all day tomorrow," he said to Franklin. "I look forward to seeing you again."

Stunned, Franklin could only nod and slowly walk out of the house.

Bud closed the door securely behind him, then turned his gaze on me. "So, what aren't you telling me that I should know?"

Chapter Twenty-one

A lot!

I almost said it, but before I could Van put his hand on my shoulder and when I turned to look at him, he shook his head. Then he turned to Bud.

"Nothing at all," he said meeting Bud's eyes and then slowly looking around the room. "We're probably all a little freaked out about the ghost, that's all."

Then he mouthed the word "bugs."

Bud's eyes widened in understanding, and he nodded back. Then he replied loudly. "Well, that makes sense," he said. "Ya'll are more nervous than a long-tailed cat in a room full of rocking chairs."

"Well, let's get searching," I said. "Then we can get out of here."

"What cha'll looking for?" Grammy asked me.

"Well, I think first we're looking for the money you hid away for the boys," I said, keeping my voice low. "Bud is going to need it to post their bail."

"And get paid," Grammy added.

I nodded. "Yes, and get paid," I agreed.

"Well, I hid the money in a place where I knew that good-for-nothing father of theirs wouldn't look," she said with a cackle. "And, come to think of it, them boys sure didn't seem too inclined in that direction either."

"So, where is it?" I asked.

She cackled again. "Nothing I love better than a good puzzle," she said. "I've done given you the clue. Now you all find the money."

Then she disappeared.

Sighing, I turned to the men and shook my head. "Okay, it seems that Grammy Anderson likes to play games," I sighed, my annoyance clear for all to see. "So, she's given me a clue to where we can find the money, and then she disappeared."

"What about the files?" Van asked.

"I didn't even get a chance to ask her about those," I admitted. "All I got was clues for the money."

"Okay, I love puzzles," Kyle said. "What's the clue?"

"She said that she hid the money in a place where their good-for-nothing father wouldn't look and then she added that the boys didn't seem too inclined in that direction either."

"That's not much of a clue," Van said. "That money could be anywhere on the property."

"Right?!?" I agreed. "We don't even know anything about the father, much less the boys."

"Wait. Wait," Kyle said, slowly walking around the room, kicking trash out of his way as he moved. "We do know that they were both living like slobs. We know they didn't clean up after themselves."

"So, they wouldn't be too inclined to use cleaning supplies?" I asked.

"Right!" Kyle exclaimed. "So, where do you put cleaning supplies?"

"Under the kitchen sink?" I suggested.

"Under the bathroom sink," Van added. "But I really don't want to have to search their bathroom."

"In the broom cupboard," Bud said.

"Oh, I like that idea the best," I replied.

We all made our way through the living room into the small kitchen. There was an old porcelain sink with a drainboard, that might have been charming at one time, but was now covered in dirty dishes and filth. There was a red and white Formica kitchen table with matching vinyl chairs, but the chairs were slashed, and stuffing was oozing out of the cuts. The old cabinets had sprung doors that hung drunkenly off their hinges. The wood floor was thick with grime and the oven had a coating of brown grease over its former white ceramic exterior.

"This place is disgusting," I said. "And I don't see a broom cupboard anywhere."

Bud moved past me to a door at the far end of the room.

"Probably the way down to the basement," Kyle called. "Or a mudroom."

126

"This whole house is a mudroom," Van said.

Bud nodded and opened the door. "It's a mudroom," he called, reaching out to pull down on the string dangling from an exposed light bulb. "And it has a cupboard."

We all hurried across the room to help. The mudroom was constructed of bare wood walls and a rough-hewn wood floor. There was a bench on one wall and some hooks on the back wall. The other wall held a door made of beadboard with a small iron handle.

Bud opened the door, and we could immediately smell the distinct scent of mice. I looked down and saw that the string mop had become a mouse hotel. "Well, no one has mopped the floor for a while," I said.

The entire cupboard was made of beadboard with two shelves above the nails used for hanging the broom, the mop, and the carpet beater.

Kyle picked up the carpet beater. "My grannie had one of these," he said fondly. "I don't think she ever used it for the carpet."

127

Bud chuckled. "Kept you in line, did she?" he asked.

"Me and the rest of the neighborhood," he replied.

Van moved the broom and the mop out of the cupboard and started knocking on the back panel, listening for hollow sounds. Bud and Kyle started to empty the shelves by handing me the boxes and containers of cleaning products.

"There might be a hidden drawer in the shelves," Bud explained.

I took the containers and started laying them on the bench, and then I thought about Momma and her safe. Grammy wouldn't hide things in secret walls or hidden compartments, she'd hide them like Momma in plain sight.

I looked at the containers I'd just placed on the bench. In the middle of them was a bright green oversized tin of 20 Mule Team Brand Borax. The little label on the front said it was sweet-smelling laundry and for household use.

"That's the last thing those boys would use," I mused.

I picked up the container, pried the lid off the top, and gasped when I saw the piles of bills stacked side-by-side inside the tin.

The men all turned when they heard my gasp.

"Winner, winner, chicken dinner," Bud said, taking the tin from me. He reached in, pulled out one pile that had been rubber-banded together, and flipped through it. "These are one-hundred-dollar bills and I'm guessing there's a hundred bills in each stack."

Chapter Twenty-two

"How many stacks are in there?" Kyle asked.

Bud shook the contents out on the bench. "Well, damn," he exclaimed softly, as the piles fell onto the wood.

"I'm estimating about $300,000," Van said.

"Yep, that's what I'm thinking too," Bud agreed.

Grammy Anderson appeared next to me and smiled. "Well, you're better at puzzles than I would have guessed," she said, with a pleased look on her face. "That there is $335,000. I figure it's enough to give those boys a good start."

"It's $335,000," I said. "Grammy just told me."

Bud gathered the piles up and stuck them back in the tin. "Well, Grammy, I'm going to deposit this in a bank account tomorrow morning," he said. "Just so it stays safe until your boys can use it."

He turned to me. "Now, where is she standing?" he asked. "I'd like to talk to her."

I turned to my side. "Grammy, Bud would like…"

Laughing, Grammy shook her head. "Girl, I can hear all of you," she said. "They just can't hear me. So, let the man talk. I'd like to see what he says."

"She says to go ahead and talk," I said.

Bud nodded. "Thank you, kindly," he said, looking at the space next to me. "I was wondering if you've been hanging around, watching over your two grandsons."

"A little bit, here and there, when I can," she replied.

I shared her response with Bud.

"Well, ma'am, I'm a little concerned that some unscrupulous folks might have been playing your grandsons. Giving them ideas that they normally wouldn't have come up with on their own."

"You mean like robbing a bank in the middle of the day?" Grammy asked.

"Like robbing the bank," I repeated to Bud.

131

"Exactly," Bud said. "You ever see or hear anyone talking to them like that?"

Grammy thought for a moment, then slowly nodded. "Strangest thing," she said slowly. "My boys would get home from a night of drinking, they'd pass out on the couch, and suddenly I'd hear voices talking to them. Telling them they deserved to be rich. Telling them the town owed them. Telling them it would be easy to rob the bank."

"Voices," I gasped. "At night. When the boys were drunk and passed out. Voices would tell them to rob the bank."

"So, the fact that the police were already at the bank before the robbery happened isn't such a big mystery anymore, is it?" Van said.

"They set my boys up?" Grammy asked.

"Yes, they did. They set your boys up," I replied.

"For the money?" Grammy asked.

"She wants to know if it was for the money?" I repeated.

132

Van shook his head. "I don't think anyone knew about the money," he said. "I think it was about the files."

Grammy shook her head. "My files?" she asked. "Why would anyone be concerned about my files?"

"I think your files might have incriminating evidence on a lot of important people," I replied. "People who would not only like to destroy the information about themselves but maybe use the information about others."

Grammy shook her head. "I burnt all them files."

"You burnt all the files?" I asked. "You don't have them anymore."

She cackled. "Them boys were all cooking up some crazy schemes and I didn't want to be no part of them."

"Which boys?" I asked. "Which boys were cooking up crazy schemes."

Her smile widened. "I might have just scanned all the files and downloaded them before I burned them," she teased. "Just for insurance."

I suddenly realized that even though I was the only one who could hear Grammy, if we were being bugged, someone else was hearing my side of the conversation.

"You scanned them? You saved them?" I whispered excitedly. "Where are they?'

She laughed. "I always did like a good puzzle," she said, then she disappeared.

Chapter Twenty-three

I turned to face Van, Kyle, and Bud.

"What?" Kyle asked. "What did she say?"

"She said she always did like a good puzzle," I sighed. "And then she disappeared."

"Even though she called me a pretty man," Kyle said, "I am getting a little impatient with that woman."

"Do you think she'll be coming back?" Bud asked.

I shrugged. "She only reappeared because we solved the first puzzle," I said. "So, I don't see her coming back, at least not tonight."

Bud nodded slowly, then surveyed our surroundings again. "Okay, well, let's just call it a night," he said loudly. "I'll come back tomorrow night and see if I can find anything more."

"But…" I began, starting to protest. Then Van turned me towards him, winked, and motioned with his head towards where the cars were parked.

Duh! There was a chance the house was bugged. How could I forget?

I rolled my eyes and mouthed my apology.

Van shook his head. "Considering the day you've had," he whispered. "I'm impressed that you're still standing upright."

"Thanks," I whispered back, feeling a little bit better.

We left the building, Bud making sure the house was locked up nice and tight, then we made our way back to the vehicles.

"So, can we meet at your place?" Bud asked. "Is it safe?"

"Why don't we meet at my place," Van suggested. "I have a feeling that Franklin might be watching L.J.'s place."

I nodded. "Besides, my place is bugged too," I said with a casual shrug.

"What?" Bud asked. "What the hell is going on here?"

I started to speak, but Bud held up his hands to stop me. "No, don't say anything until we get to Van's place," he said. "I'll want to take notes."

"Okay," I agreed. "We'll see you there."

I climbed into Van's truck and leaned back in the seat, closing my eyes for just a moment. Van leaned over and pulled my seatbelt over me, clicking it in place. I opened my eyes and smiled at him. "Thanks."

"We could do this tomorrow," he suggested, gently moving a stray hair from my forehead. "I could call…"

"No," I sighed softly. "I wouldn't be able to sleep tonight if we didn't meet."

Van chuckled. "I believe you would be asleep before your head hit your pillow," he argued gently.

"Well, it wouldn't be a good sleep because I'd be going over everything in my head," I replied. "I'd rather just get some things settled tonight."

"Okay," he said, pressing a tender kiss against my lips. "Why don't you just close your eyes for a bit while I drive, okay?"

"Yeah," I replied through a yawn. "That'd be nice."

I closed my eyes, just for a second, and when I opened them again, we were pulling down the long drive to Van's house.

"How did that..." I sputtered.

Van grinned. "Yeah, I can see that you wouldn't be able to sleep if we didn't meet," he teased. "You demonstrated that perfectly for the last fifteen minutes."

"I am so embarrassed," I muttered. Then a mortifying thought crossed my mind. I really hope I didn't snore. "I'm sorry I didn't stay awake and talk with you, so you could stay awake."

He shrugged. "No problem," he said, pulling to a stop next to the house. "I couldn't have slept anyway."

He unlocked his seatbelt, opened his door, and stepped out of the truck.

I quickly checked my face for any signs of sleep drool, thankfully there was none there. Van opened my door right after I finished patting my face down. I turned and smiled at him. "So, why couldn't you have slept?" I asked.

He studied me and then he smiled widen. "Well, bless your heart, you're afraid that you snored, aren't you?"

"No!" I lied, unsuccessfully. I paused for only a moment before I asked, "Well, did I?"

He shook his head. "No, you didn't," he said, then his voice gentled. "It was like having Sleeping Beauty resting next to me. You're beautiful when you sleep, L.J."

I got all warm and fuzzy inside again. I don't know if I'm going to ever get used to how he makes me feel. I leaned forward to slip into his arms just as Bud and Kyle pulled up right behind us.

Sighing, I climbed down onto the driveway and shrugged. "Raincheck?" I asked.

He smiled and nodded. "Deal."

139

Chapter Twenty-four

In a matter of minutes, we were all gathered around the table in the sunroom, sipping on sweet tea and nibbling on sugar cookies, courtesy of Bea.

"So," Bud said slowly, wiping his hands on a dainty linen napkin and opening up his notebook. "I think we all should get started, seeing how late it is."

I took a deep breath and nodded. "Okay, well, first…"

Bud held up his hand to stop me. "Wait. Wait just a minute, darling," he said. "Y'all have a dollar?"

Okay, I was really confused. Why in the world would he stop me, just after he said we should start, and ask me for a dollar?

"I beg your pardon?" I asked.

"Do you have a dollar?" Bud asked.

I shrugged and reached for my purse. "I'm sure…"

"Oh, I do," Bea offered, rising from her chair. "Just let me go get my sugar bowl…"

"No," Bud said to Bea. "But thank you kindly. I need a dollar from Louella Jo."

"Oh," I said slowly as I opened my billfold and pulled out a dollar bill. "You need me to pay you, so you are now working for me."

He smiled, like a proud teacher, and nodded. "Exactly," he said, reaching across the table for the bill and sliding it into his shirt pocket. "Now that you are a client, everything you say is subject to attorney-client privilege, and I can keep whatever we say confidential." He winked at me. "No matter who does the asking."

"That's brilliant," Kyle said with an approving smile. "Bud is just so brilliant."

Bud chuckled and shook his head. "Don't know about that," he replied. "But I have been around the block a few times. Now, young lady, why don't you tell me your story now."

141

I felt a little like I was in a play because I basically repeated to Bud everything I'd told the ladies at the salon this afternoon.

As I spoke, Bud took copious notes, raised his eyebrows in surprise a number of times, and actually dropped his pen on the table when I told him about the night at the beach when Deputy Hill was killed.

He didn't react nearly as much when I told him about finding Hill's body in the hole in front of the old Crenshaw Mansion. He just nodded and kinda smiled with satisfaction.

I finished with the events in the bank this evening, then I sat back in my chair, took a long drink of sweet tea, and waited to see what he had to say.

Before he spoke, he looked over his notes, tapping his pen softly on the table as he read. Finally, he exhaled softly and lifted his eyes to meet mine. "Well, things went to hell in a handbasket pert-near as you stepped off that airplane, didn't it?"

I smiled and nodded. "Pert-near," I agreed.

142

He smiled back at me and leaned back in his chair. "So, what I'm thinking here, is we got to separate and evaluate our goals and opportunities," he said.

"Okay," I replied, not really understanding what he meant.

"You have no idea what I mean, right?" he asked with a grin.

"Right," I confessed.

He chuckled again. "Okay, I see I need to put the fodder where the calf can get it."

Kyle shook his head. "Yeah, that didn't help either," he admitted.

Bud laughed out loud. "I need to explain myself clearly," Bud explained.

I nodded eagerly. "Yes, that would be good," I said.

"You don't just have one issue here," Bud said. "You have a whole load of issues. And we need to separate each one and decide how and if we want to pursue them."

Van shook his head. "No, we have one issue. The Sons of Mississippi," he argued. "We take them down, everything is resolved."

"Right. And that's the way a man in your former position would look at this problem," Bud replied. "But Louella Jo does not have the same goals as the F.B.I. Seems to me Louella Jo has three main goals. Find out who killed her momma, not just the who, but the person behind the who. Which means she needs to somehow get Congressman Patterson arrested for that murder. Then she wants to find out what happened to Amanda Lee and hopefully get her out of the situation she's in. And, finally, I have a feeling she'd like to find out who killed Sheriff King. After that, she can wash her hands of the whole deal."

"But what about the secret room?" I asked. "What about the portfolio with the names? What about the blood sacrifices?"

"Listen, I can talk to some folks I know and get a warrant to check for blood and DNA evidence on

144

Patterson's boat," Bud said. "And I can probably get ballistic tests run on Patterson's guns to see if any match the bullet that killed Sheriff King. And I can even get camera footage of the boat in the dock that carried off Amanda Lee. But taking on the whole Sons of Mississippi organization? Are you really sure you want to do that?"

Chapter Twenty-five

Do I really want to do that?

I would really like to say that I pounded my fist on the table in front of me and shouted something like, "Hell yes! I'm ready to bring those boys down!"

But I didn't. I sat there and I could feel everyone's eyes on me as I stared down at the table for a long time.

Did I really want to take on this secret order? This group that has killed people for a long time? This group that has connections all over the country including in law enforcement and politics? This group that has a dead man lying in a watery grave and a demon guarding an old mansion?

I wondered if I was strong enough. I wondered if I was brave enough.

I knew that right now, at this moment, I was tired to the depths of my soul. Did I even have it in me to fight this kind of fight?

Maybe Bud was right. Maybe all I needed to do was right those few wrongs and that would be enough.

I lifted my head, avoiding the eyes of the others, and just looked at Bud. "I don't know," I said quietly, feeling a little ashamed. "I don't know what I want to do."

"But L.J.," Van began.

"Leave her be," Bea interrupted. "This is a decision that she has to make, on her own. Because she is the one who is going to have to live with it."

I pushed my chair back and stood. "I need a minute," I said, suddenly feeling closed in.

"I'll go with…" Van offered.

I turned to him and shook my head. "No. Thank you, but no," I replied gently but firmly. "I really need a couple of minutes alone."

I walked out of the sunroom and through the house, letting myself out through the side door. I walked ahead in the soft twilight into Bea's kitchen garden. It had a small stone half-wall and a gravel path that wound through a myriad of small patches of various herbs. I

147

wandered slowly, my mind in a whirl until I came to a small stone bench and sat down.

"This was my favorite place to sit and think."

I looked up to see Myrtle standing next to me. She was dressed all in white and had a serene look on her face.

"Why here?" I asked.

She sat down next to me, and her presence sent a shiver down my spine. "Possum walking over your grave?" she asked with a smile.

I shook my head. "No, a spirit sat next to me on a bench," I replied ironically.

"Chamomile," she replied.

Okay, now I'm confused, again.

"What?"

"I sat here because it's where the chamomile grows," she said slowly as if she were talking to someone with a very low IQ. "It's that tall, spindly plant with the little daisy-like flowers on it."

I turned and leaned forward because the flowers were only a few inches away and inhaled. The scent was a

148

little sweet and earthy, but mostly it was calming. Immediately calming. I inhaled again, deeply.

"Be careful," Myrtle warned. "You don't want them to find you curled up on the path sound asleep."

I sighed and looked straight ahead. "I don't know if they'd even come looking," I admitted. "I think I disappointed them all."

"You don't give them, or yourself, enough credit," she admonished gently.

I turned to look at her. "You always seemed so sure, so confident," I said. "And I'm afraid. I admit it, I'm afraid."

"You'd be a fool not to be afraid," she replied. "You have seen them kill, you have seen them use their power to intimidate, and you have seen the great evil that influences them. If you weren't afraid, I'd think there was something wrong with you."

"So, what should I do?" I asked.

She smiled and slowly shook her head. "Oh, no, child," she said. "I am not going to make the decision for you. This is one you need to make on your own."

"No," I said, shaking my head. "This is too big a choice for me to make. I don't trust myself."

"You are the only one that can make it. You're going to have to trust yourself."

"How?" I asked. "How do I make this kind of decision?"

Myrtle was silent for a few moments, then she sighed softly. "I can tell you what I do," she said. "Then it's up to you to see if that works for you."

I nodded.

"I sit down and list all of the pros and cons I can think of, on either side of the argument," she said. "Then I weigh everything I've written down very carefully. And then I make a decision."

"That's it?" I asked, disappointed.

"And then I take it to God," she finished.

"God?" I asked, dismayed. "But I don't even know God."

She smiled at me and shook her head. "That's all right, child. He knows you."

And then she disappeared.

Chapter Twenty-six

Don't you hate it when the conversation stops as you walk into a room?

All the eyes that turned to me had questions in them. Questions that I'm sure they wanted me to answer. Questions that I didn't have the answers to.

I shrugged.

"I don't know what I'm going to do," I admitted. "I guess, at this point, I'm going to just move forward and take each day as it comes."

Bud shook his head. "That's not a plan I would advise," he said.

I nodded. "Yeah, I agree, it's not a great plan," I said. "But right now, it's all I've got. So, I've got to go with it."

"Seat of your pants planning," Kyle said with an encouraging smile. "It's spontaneous, it's creative, it's freewheeling, and it's…"

"Dangerous," Van inserted, holding my gaze with a serious look in his eyes. "Very dangerous. Because, since you don't know what you're planning, the bad guys are going to assume the worst."

"Well, even if I had made a decision, wouldn't the bad guys still be assuming the worst?" I asked.

"We could use the bugs they planted to telegraph your intentions," Van replied.

Suddenly, I was really confused.

"Wait, I thought you wanted me to help take the Sons of Mississippi down," I asked. "Right?"

He shook his head. "I want you safe," he said. "When I told you on the beach that I was in, I told you it was to keep you safe. I understand what Bud is saying, this next level, taking down the organization, it's dangerous."

"And you don't think I can do it?" I asked, hating myself for my insecurities.

Van stood up and came around the table to take my hands in his. "I think you have proven over these last

153

few weeks that you can pretty much do anything you set your mind on," he replied earnestly. "I believe that Myrtle said you were given special gifts to help you with this quest. I believe that you have enough courage and intelligence to meet any obstacle placed in your path. But you need to make that decision yourself."

He sighed slowly. "Bud is right," he said. "I saw the big picture, not the smaller ones. I'll support whatever decision you make."

I studied him for a moment. "And if I back out, will you back out?" I asked.

I saw the flash of regret in his eyes and then resolve. "That's not something that should affect your decision," he said quietly.

But I already knew. He wouldn't back out. He would continue to pursue this investigation, something he hadn't wanted to be a part of until I pulled him into it.

I turned to Bud. "How do you know that I can do the smaller goals without getting involved with taking down the whole organization?" I asked.

Bud hesitated for a moment and pondered my question. "Let's just say," he finally replied thoughtfully, "that I have some experience with organizations like these. And, for the most part, they would rather sacrifice a problematic member than have the whole organization placed at risk. If you have enough evidence to start an investigation on Patterson, they might even take care of the problem for you."

I gasped. "But that's not right. That's not how the law works," I said.

He smiled humorlessly. "But unfortunately, that's how life works," he said. "Although, we can try to protect him until his case comes to trial."

I did not want another death on my hands.

But I did not want Congressman Patterson to go free either.

And I certainly did not want Van to continue investigating all of this on his own without me. But I didn't know if I really wanted to continue investigating the Sons of Mississippi. I have to admit, they frightened me.

"Why don't you sleep on it?" Bea suggested gently. "That always helps me when I have to make decisions. A good night's sleep is what you need."

I nodded slowly. "Sleep," I repeated. "You're probably right, Bea. I need some sleep."

"Come on," Van said, slipping his arm around my shoulders and turning me toward the door. "I'll take you home."

"Thank you," I replied, my mind awhirl with thoughts. "But I probably won't sleep a wink tonight."

Chapter Twenty-seven

I can't remember what I was doing in my dream when I became aware of the magical scent of coffee subtly encroaching on my slumber. Like a drowning sailor thrashing blindly around the ocean for a lifeboat, I struggled to pull myself out of my dormant state to imbibe the lifesaving nectar of the coffee bean.

"Mmmppffhhh," I moaned.

"That's it, sweetie," Kyle crooned. "You're almost to wakey, wakey land. Just a little more."

I opened one eye and saw a blurred rendition of Kyle standing next to my bed, wafting a ceramic mug back and forth in close proximity to my face.

"Mmmmm," that sound came out as more of a whine mixed with a plea than a statement.

"No, you can't have this until you are totally awake and sitting up," Kyle replied, although I have no idea how he understood me so perfectly.

"Oooooo," I puffed.

"Now, don't get bitchy with me, young lady," he scolded. "I'm not the one who decided to sleep in until nearly eight o'clock."

"Eight o'clock!" I screamed, sitting up suddenly with both eyes wide open.

"Well, I said nearly," Kyle replied, carefully handing me the mug.

"How close is nearly?" I asked him, my eyes now slits of anger and suspicion.

"Take a sip first," Kyle suggested. "Then I'll tell you."

I sipped and as the dark, caffeinated liquid slipped through my system, I closed my eyes and sighed with contentment.

"Seven," Kyle said quickly.

My eyes popped wide open again. "What did you say?"

"I said seven," Kyle replied, not looking ashamed in the least.

"You lied to me!"

"Well, you're awake and now you have plenty of time to make yourself beautiful for your busy day at the salon," he said defensively.

"I don't need…"

"Remember, you stopped a bank robbery yesterday," he reminded me. "There are going to be reporters from all over the area following up on this human-interest story. I only have one request."

I took another sip, actually feeling better about life in general, but also, about getting up in time in particular. "And what is that?" I asked.

"If Oprah wants to interview you, I get to come too," he said.

I grinned and took another sip. "Deal," I said.

"Good," he replied, walking over to the door. "Now get your cute tush out of bed and get dressed."

He closed the door behind him, and I took one more sip and placed the mug on the nightstand beside me.

"He's so sweet," Momma said, appearing in the rocking chair in the corner of my room.

159

"He just wants to be interviewed on Oprah," I replied with a smile, sweeping the sheets to the side, getting out of bed, and walking to the bathroom.

"Have you decided?" Momma asked, gliding across the room.

I turned on the shower, undressed, and slipped under the water. "What?" I called when I could pretend I couldn't hear her.

"Funny. Funny," Momma replied. "I know you can hear me."

"I'm sorry what?" I replied as I washed my face.

"My, my, you are going to have to call the exterminator when you get a chance," Momma said. "I don't think I've ever seen a cockroach as big as that!"

"Where?" I screamed, grabbing my towel and hopping out of the tub as I searched around for the disgusting bug.

"Oh, you could hear me?" Momma replied, feigning surprise. "Why, what do you think of that."

I whipped the towel over the shower curtain bar and climbed back into the shower, washing off the soap that dripped into my eyes. "No, Momma," I said with gritted teeth. "I have not made up my mind yet."

"Good," she replied, sounding pleased.

I stuck my head out of the shower and stared at her. "Good?" I asked, surprised.

She nodded. "You take your time," she advised. "Don't be rushed into doing something you'll regret later. Make sure you feel good about your decision. Guilt is never a good reason to do something."

I stepped back under the pouring water. "Never?" I asked.

"Well, except if it has something to do with your mother," she chuckled softly. "Then guilt is always a good reason."

Chapter Twenty-eight

"Damn girl," Kyle gasped as we turned down the street toward the salon. The middle of the street was crowded with vans from various news agencies in the area. On the sidewalk and next to the curb were at least a dozen sets of reporters with their camera operators.

Kyle pulled to the curb at the end of the block, then turned to me. "Okay, we can do this the wrong way or the right way," he said.

Slightly exasperated, I rolled my eyes. "Oh, let's do it the wrong way this time," I said sarcastically.

Kyle grinned. "Oh, you thought that all this stuff you've been doing lately has been the right way?" he asked. "Sorry, my mistake."

I snorted. I couldn't help myself.

"Okay, my PR consultant, how should I handle this?" I asked.

"That's better," he replied. "Much better." He smiled with satisfaction and then inhaled softly before he

162

began. "Okay, if we drive up to the front of the salon, there are going to be a bunch of photographs of you pushing your way through the crowd to get to the salon. And then, photos of you unlocking the door – you know, those butt shots we all adore."

I shook my head. "Stuff of my nightmares," I said. "What's behind door number two?"

"We drive around back," Kyle said. "We unlock the back door, turn on the lights to the salon. You go to the front of the salon, graciously open the door, positioning yourself so your logo shows behind you, and welcome the questions."

"I really like Plan B," I said. "And I'm assuming that was the right way, right?"

Kyle sighed loudly. "I have no idea what you would do without me."

He slowly backed the car up, made a U-turn, and then pulled around through the alley to the back of the salon. We parked between the dumpster and the back door, slipped out of the car, and quickly unlocked the door.

"I wondered when you were going to get here," Maribelle said from the backroom as she filled up the coffeemaker. "Seems like you're a celebrity. So, what did you do?"

"What did she do?" Ida gasped as she hurried into the room and closed the door behind her. "Why she stopped a bank robbery last night. That's what she did."

"You did what?" Maribelle asked.

"It wasn't that..." I began, then I realized that Ida had come in through the front of the shop. "Ida, how did you get in?"

"Oh," Ida replied, a little disconcerted. "I didn't realize...I thought they would just let me..." She sighed. "I sort of let them in."

I turned to Kyle. "What should I..."

Kyle shrugged and rolled his eyes. "Why do I have to take care of everything?" he asked dramatically.

"Just stay back here, darling. I'll let you know when your people are ready for you."

He strode out of the room and his voice carrying over the clamor of the reporters. "People. People. Please, let's have a little bit of order here," he insisted. "I know you want to speak with Ms. Carter, and I assure you, she wants to speak with you. But we really need to organize ourselves a little better, don't you think?"

The door opened behind me and Cici hurried in, nearly invisible behind the stacks of white pastry boxes she was carrying.

"Cici, what in the…"

"There have never, ever been so many reporters in Julep," she said, placing her boxes on the counter. "And there has never been an opportunity like this for me to advertise my bakery." She turned pleading eyes on me. "You wouldn't mind…"

"No, of course not," I said.

"Wait just a minute," Maribelle inserted. "One of these boxes is for us, right?"

165

Cici chuckled. "Well, of course," she said, slipping a box off the top. "And I left the calories at the bakery."

Then she picked up the rest of the boxes and moved toward the door. "Good luck with your interviews, cher," she said, bustling forward into the salon. "Good morning, these pastries are compliments of Cici's Bakery just down the street. Please, help yourselves."

Maribelle opened the box Cici left, lifted out a chocolate éclair, and held it up to her face. "Welcome to lifestyles of the rich and fattening," she said with a sigh, then took a big bite out of it.

Chapter Twenty-nine

I watched as the last reporter, a high-heeled, blonde-haired, modelesque beauty, made her way towards the front door of the salon, then, at the last moment, she turned and jogged back to the counter, the clacking of her heels against the tile floor echoing in the room. She reached in and pulled out a crème-filled pastry and sighed, "I know I'm going to regret this," she said. "But I just can't resist."

She stuffed her microphone under her arm, wrapped the pastry in a napkin, and click-clacked out the door.

As soon as she was gone, I collapsed into the chair at Kyle's station and sighed, "Can I go home now?"

I rubbed my jaw, aching from all the smiles I'd offered during the past thirty minutes.

"Go home?" Kyle retorted. "Oh, honey, your day is just beginning."

I sighed and nodded. "Okay, Ida," I exhaled slowly. "When's my first appointment?"

"Are you kidding me?" Ida asked. "I called up and pushed back everyone's schedule for the next hour, so you can tell us just what happened last night."

Maribelle smiled and nodded. "Good for you, Ida," she said, slipping into her own station's chair. "Well, spill it, boss lady."

I started to get out of Kyle's chair when he placed his hand on my shoulder and shook his head. "Oh, no, you need the seat of honor," he said. "I'll sit here."

He slipped up onto the counter, leaned forward, put his elbows on his knees, his head in his hands, and turned to look at me. "Well. We're waiting."

"It was not really that big of a deal," I began. "I just did what I thought was right."

"Oh, girlfriend, don't play it off," Kyle exclaimed, then he turned to the rest of the group. "Two masked men with guns pointed at her and she says it's not that big of a deal."

168

"Guns?" Georgia exclaimed. "They had guns pointed at you and you didn't just faint. Girl, if you had balls, they would be made of steel."

"Actually," I began, feeling uncomfortable with all the attention. "I wouldn't have done a thing if Kyle hadn't stepped between a hysterical woman and one of the bank robbers."

"You did what?" Kasey asked.

Kyle shrugged. "It was nothing."

"Mmmm-hmmmm," I said, rolling my eyes. "She was crying, and the robber was freaking out and pointing his gun at her. Then Kyle just subtly steps between them, getting her out of range and tries to calm everyone down."

"We've got two heroes in the house," Maribelle said.

Kyle looked uncomfortable. Good! Now he can see what it feels like.

"I just…"

"Did what you thought was right?" I asked with a grin.

169

He grinned. "Bitch," he mouthed at me.

"So, what happened next?" Ida asked.

I shrugged. "Then the ghost of Grammy Anderson shows up in the middle of this whole charade," I said. "Telling me to deliver a message to her grandsons – the bank robbers."

"Grammy Anderson?" Ida exclaimed. "Why she was my momma's third cousin twice removed."

Kyle looked at Ida and shook his head. "What in the hell does that even mean?" he asked.

Ida laughed. "It just means that we're related," she said. "In a distant kind of way. I met her several times at family reunions. You always wanted to get a piece of her fried chicken at the picnic. No one could touch her recipe." Ida sighed. "I would kill for that recipe."

"Too late," Kyle said. "She's already dead."

"I didn't mean that," Ida said, horrified. "I just meant…" Then she realized that Kyle was teasing. "Oh, you. You were just joshing me."

"So, the bank robbers were Jasper and LeRoy?" Georgia asked.

I nodded. "Yes, do you know them?"

"Jasper went to school with my little sister," she explained. "His momma died young, and his daddy was a snake in the grass. Grammy Anderson raised both of them boys and raised 'em good. Went to church every Sunday. Did well enough at school."

"So, what happened to them?" Kyle asked.

"Grammy died," Georgia said. "Only thing holding them together I suppose. She was the motivating force in their lives. Neither boy had much in the brains department."

Ida nodded. "Didn't have the sense God gave a goose," she added.

"So, they could be easily persuaded to do something?" Kyle asked. "You don't think they could come up with the idea to rob the bank?"

Georgia snorted. "Honey, if either of those boys had an idea, it would die of loneliness," she said. "The porch light's on, but no one is at home."

I glanced over at Kyle and nodded. "Yeah, we kind of got that impression too," I said. "We think someone put them up to it – and wanted them to get caught."

"Why?" Kasey asked.

"Probably so they could find them files Grammy Anderson had on all the folks in town," Ida chimed in.

Surprised, Kyle and I stared at Ida. "How did you..."

"You learn a lot at family reunions," she said with a smile like a Cheshire cat. "Specially if you're trying to be invisible while you're sneaking seconds of banana cream pie."

Well, bless her heart.

Chapter Thirty

It felt good to be busy and it kept my mind off the decision I knew I was going to have to make...someday. I had a couple of regular customers from the Julep Senior Citizen Home for their weekly shampoo, curl up, and tease-out appointments. I loved chatting with those ladies and hearing the latest gossip about the scandalous behavior of some of the other widows living at the home.

Then I had twin boys, four years old, in for their first official haircut. Bless their hearts, it was like cutting the hair of an octopus that had been greased down like a pig. Those boys twitched and turned every which way until Maribelle offered them a sucker if they could sit still and count to one hundred. Course, being four, if I every so often started counting with them started at twenty, they would forget where they were and start counting at twenty all over again. It worked like a charm, and we were only down four suckers by the time they were done.

Ida scheduled me for some office time after that, so I could work on the books and order supplies. I cleaned up my station, swept up the blonde locks from the twins, hung my apron on the hook next to the chair, and headed toward the back room. I was really looking forward to closing the door and sipping on an ice-cold soda.

But, as soon as I cracked open the can of soda, there was a knock on the office door. I sighed silently.

Yes?" I called out.

Ida opened the door a crack. "There's someone here to see you," she whispered, her eyes wide with concern.

"An appointment?" I asked.

She shook her head. "No," she said softly. "It's him. That trooper fella."

"Franklin?" I asked, surprised.

She nodded frantically. "Shall I tell him you're not here?" she asked.

"No, that's all right," I replied. "I can talk to him."

"Well, that's a relief." Franklin's voice sounded just behind Ida, and she jumped and let out a little scream.

"What are you doing here?" she demanded, turning and blocking the door.

"Waiting to speak to Louella Jo," he replied impatiently.

"Well, don't get your knickers in a knot," she replied haughtily. "She said she'd talk to you, so you might as well go on in."

Franklin entered the small office and his presence seemed to make the office shrink in size. Then Ida stuck her head in, gave Franklin a sour look, and then turned to me. "I'll be back to check in on you in a little bit," she said, then she closed the door behind her.

I bit back a smile, then I turned to Franklin. "Pull up a chair," I said, motioning to the only other chair in the room.

He glanced at the door. "I don't think she likes me," he said.

"She's just very protective," I replied with an easy shrug.

He sat down, his hat clasped in his hands, and leaned forward. "Why would she feel like she needed to be protective, Louella Jo?" he asked. "I thought we were friends."

I leaned back in my chair and studied him. He obviously wasn't the same old Franklin I knew in high school, and I certainly wasn't the same old Louella Jo from back then. But can a person's character change as much as their appearance?

I sighed. Well, the least I could do is be honest with him.

"Franklin, we were friends," I said. "Good friends. Best friends. But lately, when I talk to you, I feel like there's another agenda on your mind. I feel like you're watching my words, waiting for me to slip up. I probably should be asking you the same question. Why don't you trust me?"

He nodded slowly. "That's fair," he said. "That's real fair. I haven't been honest with you, and I have treated you like you were a suspect and not a friend."

Hmmm, is this one of those good cop - bad cop scenarios? Is he playing me?

He paused for a moment, then smiled sadly. "What are you thinking?"

"I'm wondering if you're trying to play me," I replied honestly. "One of those good cop – bad cop deals. Except, you know, usually in those circumstances you don't get one person to try and play both roles."

He chuckled softly and then sat back in his chair. "Yeah, I could see how you might take my actions that way," he agreed. Then he shrugged and looked at me. I could see something in his eyes that made me feel uneasy.

Finally, he replied, "And that's certainly less embarrassing than the truth."

"What's the truth?" I asked, regretting the words as soon as they left my mouth.

"I believe I'm still in love with you, Louella Jo," he said quietly. "And at first I was trying to impress you with my newfound detective skills. Then…" He sighed. "Then I was jealous and didn't handle it well at all."

"Franklin, I…"

He shook his head. "No, don't say anything," he said. "I can see that there's something between you and Van."

He stood up, walked over to my chair, leaned down in front of me, and then placed his hand on the back of my chair, his face only inches away from mine.

I have to admit, that I suddenly found it very difficult to breathe in that little room.

"Franklin," I breathed.

He reached down with his other hand and gently rubbed his thumb across my lips. "I can't tell you how many times I've dreamt about you whispering my name like that," he confessed.

I leaned back, breaking contact with his thumb, and slowly shook my head. My heart was breaking for him, but not because of him. "I can't…"

He leaned closer. "Louella Jo, I didn't lose all this weight, put on all this muscle, and get where I am today by taking no for an answer," he said. Then he leaned forward and pressed his lips against mine.

"How about hell no?" Van asked from the doorway.

Chapter Thirty-one

Why in the world was I feeling guilty?

I did absolutely nothing wrong.

So why was I blushing and feeling like a kid who just got caught with her hand in the cookie jar?

I reached up and pushed against Franklin's shoulders, trying to move him away from me. But I was about as successful as a leaf in the wind. Franklin took his time releasing my lips and when he lifted his head, I could see a gleam of pure masculine triumph in his eyes.

And that's when embarrassment turned into anger. So, just as Franklin was turning his triumphant smile towards Van, in that unguarded moment of victory, I closed my hand into a tight fist and punched him for all I was worth, right into his solar plexus.

"Ooooph!" Franklin wheezed, a look of total shock replacing his smile.

I stood up quickly, my chair falling back behind me. "How about taking that for an answer?" I spat.

180

Franklin wheezed and stumbled back a few steps.

Van stepped up and steadied him. "Okay, buddy, just bend over and take a few deep breaths," he instructed, not trying very hard to hide the amusement on his face.

"How's your fist feel, champ?" he asked me.

I shrugged. "Fine," I said, flexing all of my fingers to make sure. "No damage at all."

Franklin wheezed again.

"Yeah, you just keep working on those deep breaths," Van said. "And you'll feel better in no time."

Van looked back at me. "Solar plexus, huh?" he asked.

I nodded, standing tall with my hands on my hips. "Self-defense class, Greenwich YWCA," I replied.

"You know you just assaulted an officer of the law," Van added casually.

Franklin inhaled sharply.

"Are you going to press charges?" I asked Franklin.

181

He shook his head and inhaled slowly again. Then he slowly straightened himself up and met my eyes. "I deserved that," he breathed. "I acted like an ass."

I nodded. "Yes, you did," I agreed.

"Truce?" he asked.

"Sure," I said with a curt nod. "But if you try that again..."

He put his hands up in the air. "I won't try that again," he assured me. Then he smiled. "But it was worth it, Louella Jo. It was surely worth it."

He turned, then straightened up a little more, and slowly, painfully walked out of the office, closing the door behind him.

"You still mad?" Van asked, walking over to the door and locking it.

I exhaled slowly and nodded. "Yeah, just a little," I admitted. "I thought he was actually trying to be friends. I thought he was trying to build up a little trust here."

Van stepped closer and placed his hands on my shoulders. "Maybe he was," he suggested. "Maybe he started out with good intentions."

"Well, starting out isn't good enough," I fumed. "He needs to follow through."

Van grinned. "Seems to me he was following through," he said, gently massaging my shoulders. "In some ways, I feel sorry for the guy."

"Sorry?" I asked incredulously. "Sorry?"

Van leaned forward and gently kissed me.

"That's not going to..." I murmured against his lips.

Then he pulled me against him and deepened the kiss, sliding his hands up to cradle my head as he plundered my mouth. I moaned softly and returned the kiss, passion for passion. My hands slipped into his hair holding his mouth in place, my mind was in a tumult of emotion, my body in an electrifying meltdown.

The knock on the door came from miles away and didn't register at first. Then it was repeated, this time with more force.

"Louella Jo, are you okay in there?" Ida called frantically.

Van released me and I stumbled back and perched on the edge of the deck.

"Fine," I gasped, but my voice was too breathy for it to carry.

I cleared my throat and tried again.

"I'm fine, Ida," I said, my voice still a little shaky. "Franklin left a few minutes ago."

Van reached up and tenderly stroked my heated cheek. I trembled at both his touch and the look in his eyes as he stepped closer.

"Well, your next appointment is here," Ida called through the door, cooling the passion I was feeling. "A few minutes early, but I told her that you would be right out."

An odd mixture of disappointment and relief swept through my body. My reaction to Van terrified me, but when I wasn't thinking about it and just enjoying it – it was amazing. But, maybe, just maybe, retreat was the better side of valor in this situation.

Van dropped his hand and nodded. "Go get 'em, Champ," he whispered, stepping back.

I inhaled a deep shaky breath and nodded. "Yeah, thanks, I will."

Chapter Thirty-two

I was grateful for my busy schedule for the rest of the afternoon. I didn't want to have time to think about anything that wasn't directly related to hair styling.

I didn't want to think about the decision I was going to have to make.

I didn't want to think about what Franklin said.

And I certainly didn't want to think about Van and what he did to my emotions.

I sighed slowly.

Dammit! I was thinking about him again.

"You got man problems, honey?"

I looked into the mirror and met Miss Elsie's eyes. Miss Elsie was the last of my customers from the Senior Home. She was nearly one hundred years old. I say nearly because no one, including Miss Elsie herself, knew how old she actually was. In the 1920s, when she was born, midwives came to southern rural homes to assist with childbirth and many of those births never got recorded.

I ran a comb through her thick, white hair and nodded slowly. "How could you tell?" I asked as I trimmed off less than a quarter-inch of hair.

"Oh, honey," she cackled. "Ain't nothing like a man can bring that look of consternation into a woman's face."

"Right?" I agreed, sliding the comb through another section, and trimming off a little more hair.

"So, what'cha gonna do about it?" she asked.

I shook my head. "I have no idea," I replied honestly. "I seem to lose my ability to think when he's nearby."

She chuckled and her eyes twinkled with mischief. "Oh, I remember those days," she said. "My Vernon," She sighed loudly. "That man could heat me up faster than an iron griddle on a wood stove."

She sighed again.

"Do you miss him?" I asked.

Her eyes softened and she nodded. "Every day," she said. "Every single day. And it doesn't get any easier."

187

I shook my head. "So, it's not worth it. You end up sad and lonely."

"Oh, child, no," she said. "No, you don't understand. Let me explain it to you."

She lifted her hands out from under the black salon cape she was wearing. Her hands were large and wrinkled, with age spots scattered across the top, and veins so clear under the thin, paper-like skin that you could count them.

"See these hands?" she asked.

I nodded.

"These ain't pretty model hands, are they?"

I didn't want to be rude, so I made a noncommittal shrug.

She cackled softly. "Oh, honey, I know they aren't soft and pretty," she said. "And I used to long for soft and pretty hands. You know, with the fancy nails and the plump, fine skin. And the tiny knuckles that you could barely see."

I glanced at her knuckles. They were large and rough.

"These hands," she continued. "These hands are like my heart. Iffen I wanted to, I could have kept them nice and safe, covered up from harsh weather, hard work, or scratches and bruises. But these hands…these hands held newborn babies, they comforted weeping children, they felt foreheads for fevers and patched skinned knees. These hands made dinners for new mothers, changed the sheets on sickbeds, got pricked on flower thorns for bridal bouquets, and tossed handfuls of dirt onto the tops of the caskets of my family and friends who went before me. These hands lived and served and earned every wrinkle and bump and callous they wear."

She looked up at me and her smile was luminous.

"Child, you do not want to go to your grave with a heart that hasn't been well worn," she said gently. "You want a heart that been bumped and bruised and tattered. You want a heart that's been filled with joy and overwhelmed with sadness. You want a heart that has

189

served others selflessly because that's the only kind of heart you want to bring with you when you go to heaven. There's no reward for a pretty heart, the good book says there's only a reward for a well-used and broken heart. You hear?"

"Yes ma'am," I whispered, my voice tight with emotion.

"Good," she nodded with approval, and then the twinkle was back in her eyes. "Now, what do you think about purple highlights?"

Chapter Thirty-three

Entering the bank that evening was weird. I knew that the odds of having another bank robbery at the same bank the following day were a million to one, but I still hesitated as I stepped up to the door.

"Yeah, I get you," Kyle said, reaching over and pushing the door open for me. "But we've got to face our fears."

I looked up at him. "Why?" I asked earnestly. "Why can't we just turn around and run away from our fears?"

He smiled and then shrugged. "Because then it would be too easy to keep running, for the rest of our lives," he said.

"Okay, you win," I said, and I stepped forward into the bank lobby.

Suddenly, the noise level in the lobby dropped and all eyes turned to look at me. A teller in the far window started to clap, then she was joined by the rest of the tellers and all of the depositors standing in line, who had probably been in the bank with me yesterday.

"Thank you," I murmured, as I blushed furiously. "Thank you so much."

Then the line of people standing in front of the teller in the first window stepped out of line and waved us forward, to the front.

"Now, that's what I'm talking about," Kyle whispered to me.

"Really, that's not necessary," I said, standing still.

"Please," the woman who'd been chatting about Dolly Parton with Kyle the day before insisted. "Please, it's the least we can do."

I sighed and nodded. "Thank you," I said, moving to the front of the line.

"When you're done here," the teller whispered to me when I handed her my deposit slip. "Mr. Murphy, the bank president would like to see you in his office."

"Ohhhh, maybe there's a reward," Kyle said.

"Nothing was stolen," I reminded him. "So, how could there be a reward?"

"Good point," Kyle replied.

The teller took my deposit, counted it, punched it into the computer, and then handed me my empty deposit bag along with my receipt. "His office…"

"Thanks," I interrupted politely. "I know where his office is. Have a lovely evening."

"You too," she replied with a smile. "And thank you again."

I turned away, feeling a little anxious about my meeting with Harold Murphy.

"What?" Kyle whispered.

"I'm just feeling a little apprehensive," I replied softly.

"Because he's an ass or because he's part of the Sons of Mississippi?" he asked quietly.

"Yes," I replied.

We walked across the lobby towards Mr. Murphy's office and just when I was about to knock on

193

the heavy walnut door, it opened in front of us, and Bud stepped out.

We all stood in shocked silence for a moment, then Bud seemed to get control of his senses and smiled at us. "Well, two of my most favorite people," he said with a smile that I didn't think reached all the way to his eyes.

"The teller told us that Mr. Murphy wanted to see me," I replied.

"And I'm her muscle," Kyle added.

Bud smiled at Kyle, then turned to me. "Good choice for muscle," he said. He looked back over his shoulder, then stepped out of the room and closed the door behind him. "Mr. Murphy is on the phone right now. This might not be the best time to meet with him."

"Oh, that's fine with me," I said. "I didn't want to see him in the first place."

"Besides, L.J. and I are due a movie night," Kyle said, then he sent a sideways glance at Bud. "Unless you have other ideas for the evening."

Really? Really? Kyle was going to desert me, just so he could have a fabulous evening with Bud?

I sighed.

I guess I couldn't blame him.

"Actually, I do have another idea," Bud replied. "But y'all might not be too keen on it."

"What idea?" I asked.

"Y'all want to come with me and explore the speakeasy?"

Chapter Thirty-four

"No," I said, firmly placing my hands on my hips.

"No," I repeated, straightening my back, and lifting my head slightly.

"No," I tried again, this time with pouty lips, and sucked in cheeks.

"What the hell are you doing, girl?" Kyle asked, peeking in through my open bedroom door.

I turned from my full-length mirror and glared at him. "I'm practicing saying no," I replied. "Because I obviously have a problem stating it."

He chuckled. "Well, you know, Bud is pretty charming," he said with an easy shrug. "He would've talked you into it anyway. So, look at it this way. Saying 'yes' saved us all a lot of time."

I rolled my eyes. "You're supposed to be helping me, Kyle," I said. "Me being a doormat is not going to be helpful."

Kyle walked across the room and sat on the edge of my bed. "Oh, come on, you know you wanted to explore that speakeasy just as much as I did," he said. "Think of the romance, think of the intrigue, think of the..."

"Snakes," I inserted. "And bugs, big, fat, squirmy ones."

Kyle shuddered. "Now, did you have to do that?"

I nodded. "Yes, I did," I said. "And spiders and spider webs. And probably rodents. Not cute little field mice. No, I'd bet there were big, nasty river rats..."

"That's enough!" Kyle cried, jumping off the bed and striding across the room towards the door.

"Where are you going?" I asked, biting back a smile.

"To change my outfit," he explained.

I looked at his sky-blue shirt, khaki slacks, and canvas loafers. I wish I could look as perfectly put together. "Why?" I asked.

He exhaled impatiently. "Well, now I'm going to have to find an outfit that will go with my combat boots," he huffed, then turned quickly and stormed out of the room.

I turned back to look at my reflection, noted the cute skinny jeans, the button-down cotton print tunic shirt, and the coordinating ballet flats, and sighed. Kicking off the flats, I knelt down in front of my closet and reached toward the back.

"What are you looking for?" Momma asked from behind me.

"My rubber boots," I called back, my voice muffled by the clothes hanging in my face.

"Which rubber boots?" she asked, and I could tell she was moving closer.

"You know, those cute little Ralph Lauren rubber boots," I replied. "They were yellow and they had a horse…"

"Oh, yes, I gave them to the church auction last year."

I pulled my head out of the closet and looked at her in disbelief. "You did what?" I asked.

"Well, I'm sure I asked you," she replied. "It was a fundraiser for hurricane relief."

"I don't remember..." I began.

"I'm sure I asked you," she insisted. "I'm sure you said that you would never wear them anyway."

I sighed. Maybe she was right.

"Now what am I supposed to do?" I asked, looking at my collection of fairly flimsy flats and heels.

"You can wear mine," Momma suggested. "They're still in my closet."

With all that had been happening, I hadn't had a chance to...

Okay, why am I lying?

The very last thing I wanted to do was go into my momma's closet and relive all of the memories associated with her things. I knew I needed a whole weekend, several boxes of facial tissues, and chocolates, lots of chocolates, in order to face that task.

199

"I don't know, Momma…" I started

She looked down at me and nodded with kindness. "Why don't I just go and get them?" she suggested.

How did she know?

"Thank you, Momma."

Just when I was all full of loving, kind, grateful, daughter-like thoughts, my momma came back with the boots and ruined them all.

"I can't wear these!" I exclaimed.

"Why not?" she asked, holding up the ugliest pair of rainboots I'd ever seen in my life.

It wasn't just that they were neon lime green. It wasn't just that they had bright orange laces up the front. It wasn't just that they had a large pattern of fuchsia cabbage roses scattered over them. To top it all off, they were trimmed with fuchsia fake fur.

"Why do they have fur?" I asked, grabbing on to just one of the objections to the boots.

"In case I need to wear them in the snow," Momma quickly responded.

"Momma, this is Julep, Mississippi. We don't get snow down here!"

"It could happen," she replied, then she grinned. "Sides, they were on sale. I saved eighty-five percent."

"You still paid too much," I muttered. I shook my head. "I just can't…"

"L.J.," Kyle yelled from the first floor. "They're just pulling up."

I looked at the boots. Then looked at my flats. Then I pictured one of the creepy crawlies that I'd been teasing Kyle about skittering over my foot and sighed. "Hand 'em over," I said, defeated.

"Please?" Momma reminded me with a raised eyebrow.

"I'm sorry," I said. "Momma, may I please borrow your rubber boots?"

"Well, of course, dear," she replied, placing them down next to me. Then she brightened. "Do you want the matching raincoat?"

A shiver of revulsion ran up my spine as I pictured the neon lime green monster. "No, Momma, thank you, but no."

Chapter Thirty-five

"Cute boots," Kyle said sarcastically, not even trying to hide his smile. "Are you trying to frighten away the creatures of the night or are you afraid you're going to get swallowed up by tall vegetation and this is the only way we'll be able to find you?"

"Just shut up," I growled, moving past him and heading to the door. "I am so not in the mood."

Van was standing alongside his truck, waiting for us. He glanced at my boots, started to open his mouth, and stopped. I swear I saw Kyle out of the corner of my eye sending him some kind of signal. But when I turned to him, his hands were at his side and a look that wouldn't melt butter was on his face.

"What?" he asked innocently.

I just glared at him and climbed into the truck.

Van closed my door after me, then came around to the other side of the vehicle, while Kyle climbed into the back seat.

"So, how was the rest of your day?" Van asked cordially as he put the truck in reverse and backed down the driveway.

I took a deep breath, tried to calm myself down, and then turned and smiled at Van. "Miss Elsie was in today," I said. "She is such a sweetheart."

He shook his head. "Miss Elsie is a state treasure," he agreed. "How is she doing?"

"She wanted purple highlights," I said, feeling the smile on my face.

"Did you talk her out of them?" he asked.

I shook my head. "Oh, no," I said. "When you get to be her age, you get to wear your hair any way you like."

"She looked so cute walking out of the salon," Kyle said. "Stopping at every station, looking at herself in the mirror, and patting her hair like a teenager."

"You made her happy," Van said with an admiring smile.

I shrugged. "Making her happy, made me happy," I replied. "Besides, she helped me with a problem, so it was the least I could do."

"What problem?" he asked, suddenly concerned.

I grinned and shook my head. "Just a lesson learned, that's all," I replied easily, and then I decided to change the subject. "So, what do you know about the speakeasy?"

"Well, Grammy Anderson ran it until about five years ago, when she started feeling poorly," he said. "One day the diner was open, the next day there was a closed sign on the door. And since you had to go through the diner to get into the speakeasy, they both were out of business."

"What happened? Why was it so fast?" Kyle asked.

"I heard she had a stroke," Van replied. "She lost movement on one side of her body, so she couldn't run it anymore. And the boys were just teenagers, they couldn't take over for her."

"So, no one offered to help her?" I asked.

"Oh, there were offers," Van said. "But she turned them all down. She didn't want anyone messing with her stuff."

I nodded slowly. "Her secrets," I suggested.

"Yeah, I think that's probably it," he agreed.

"I wonder if that's when she decided to take all the notes and scan them?" I mused aloud.

Kyle shook his head. "I'm guessing she did it before she had her stroke," he said. "Or we would have found a scanner and a computer inside the house."

"That's right," I said, surprised. "There wasn't anything like that in there. Unless someone got to them before we did."

"Don't you think she would have told you?" Van asked.

"I don't know, she really likes riddles," I replied. "All she said was that the boys were cooking up some crazy schemes and she didn't want to be a part of them."

"Were the boys her grandsons?" Kyle asked.

I shook my head. "I think if her grandsons were cooking up some crazy schemes, she would have stopped them before they even had a chance to start," I replied. "Besides, they didn't seem like the scheming type."

Kyle nodded. "More like lost puppies," he added. "Looking for someone to tell them what to do."

"Well, hopefully, we find out soon enough," Van said, as he pulled down the dark and overgrown driveway. "Because we've arrived."

Chapter Thirty-six

The diner was frozen in time. From the glitter-speckled, red Naugahyde benches and red and white swirled Formica table tops, to the condiment caddies and black and white menus, I felt as if I could just flip a switch and everything would just start moving, all of us transported back to the fifties. The days of poodle skirts, rock and roll, and muscle cars.

But that was just a façade, I reminded myself. This diner had been open until just a few years ago. But Grammy had been able to somehow capture that moment and recreate it in the diner. The small blackboard near the front door spelled out that today's special was Meatloaf Surprise, which included soup, salad, mashed potatoes, mixed vegetables, and your choice of beverage.

"What a deal," Kyle exclaimed. "All that for $5.99. You can't get a glass of water for $5.99 in New York."

"This place is amazing," I said as I slowly took it all in. "It's like a museum of small-town living. Look at the bulletin board – posters for the high school play, flyers from the churches, help wanted ads, items for sale. This is where people came, every day, to get in touch with local news."

"I remember coming in here right after the morning chores were done," Bud said. "A bunch of us farmers would meet, eat a big breakfast, and complain about the job we all loved. The whole community lost a piece of our hearts when the diner closed down."

"I had no idea."

I jumped and turned around. Grammy Anderson was standing right behind me with tears running down her translucent face. "I had no idea my little diner meant so much to them," she whispered hoarsely.

"Sounds like you made it a place where everyone felt welcome," I said. "A second home."

She smiled. "And that's what I wanted," she said. "If someone couldn't get their momma's or their granny's cooking, well then, they could have mine. I'd be their momma or granny for the night."

"That's nice," I said. "That's really nice."

"Why are y'all here?"

"We're looking for the notes," I explained. "The ones you had about your guests in the speakeasy."

"Why do you want those?" she asked. "That's old business. That's the past."

"Well, sometimes things in the past are connected to things in the present," I replied.

"And I say leave the past behind," Grammy Anderson answered. "What you're looking for is nothing but a recipe for trouble."

"Won't you help us at all?" I asked. "Just a clue."

She smiled and started to fade away. "Maybe I will and maybe I won't."

Then she disappeared.

"Grammy Anderson?" Bud asked.

I nodded. "She was really touched by your characterization of her diner," I said.

He smiled. "I was kind of hoping she would be," he admitted.

"You said all those nice things to draw her here?" I asked, surprised.

"You can catch more flies with honey than vinegar," he replied with an easy shrug. "Did she give you any clues about the files?"

I shook my head. "She said that we were looking for nothing but a recipe for trouble, going after those files," I replied. "She thought we should leave the past in the past."

"Well, if there was nothing important in those files, no one would have been going after the Anderson boys," Bud reasoned. "She just might not know what she had. But with or without her help, we need to find those files."

He walked away from me, shining his flashlight in front of him and using the counter as a guide until he came to a doorway at the corner of the room. He lifted the flashlight beam and illuminated a sign with the word

211

"Restrooms" painted on it. He turned back to us and announced, "I believe this is the way."

Kyle hurried to follow him, but I waited a moment to have a word with Van.

"What?" Van asked.

"I'm just a little troubled that he was playing on Grammy Anderson's emotions," I said. "It seemed dishonest."

Van nodded slowly. "Or it could seem like what a lawyer would use to get more information out of a suspect," he suggested.

"Okay, yeah, it could be a lawyer thing," I conceded. "But it still seemed a little…"

"Sleazy?" Van added.

"Maybe not all the way too sleazy," I said with a little bit of a smile. "But underhanded kind of fits the description for me."

"Well, think of it this way," Van said, placing his arm around my shoulders and guiding me toward the doorway that Kyle and Bud had disappeared through.

"He's doing it for a good cause."

Chapter Thirty-seven

I don't know what I was expecting, but the
sophisticated bar with soft lights, rich wood furnishings
and brass fittings, jeweled-colored upholstery, and brick-
tiled floor was not it. I guess I was thinking more like
someone's basement with a bar in the corner. This place
could have passed for one of the exclusive pubs in Boston.

"Whoa!" I breathed as I stepped down the final
step into the bar itself.

"I turned on the lights," Bud explained. "Because
this is a basement, and no one would be able to see us."

"Good thinking," Van said. "Do you have any
idea where we should start looking?"

Bud shook his head. "No, I don't," he confessed.
"There's behind the bar and all of its nooks and crannies.
There's the poker room that's behind the door to the right
of the bar. And the private party room, that's just beyond
the bar to the left."

"How about offices?" Kyle asked, slipping behind the bar. "Shouldn't there be an office for the books somewhere down here?"

He slowly moved along the mirrored wall that held shelves of liquor bottles. "Great selection," he said with admiration, and then he smiled. "Good old Jack Daniels sitting right next to Hennessy Cognac, we ain't discriminating here. A little something for every taste."

Suddenly stopping, he studied the shelves, then turned back to us. "How upset would everybody be if I tried something, and all of the bottles came tumbling down?"

Bud rushed over. "Hand me the cognac before you try it," he insisted.

Chuckling, Kyle grabbed the ornate glass bottle of cognac and placed it on the bar behind him, then turned back and pressed both hands on a piece of mirror and pushed against it. The mirror moved backward, clicked, and then opened forward to reveal a narrow door-sized opening. "Voila!" Kyle called. "The secret office."

215

I slipped behind the bar and came up next to him. I sniffed the air coming from the opening – it didn't smell stale or even moldy, like a room that had been closed up for years, it smelled more like the swamp.

"Well, are we going in?" Kyle asked, eagerly stepping through the doorway.

"How far are we away from the swamp?" I asked.

Kyle froze. "Swamp?"

"It actually backs up to the property line," Bud said. "Why?"

"Because it smells like a swamp to me," I said. "Not a closed-up room."

"Escape hatch?" Van wondered aloud, following me around the bar. "Revenue men coming down the steps and the clientele escaping out through a secret door behind the bar."

"Swamp?" Kyle repeated, stepping back into the room. "Like snakes and alligators?"

I turned my flashlight on and shined it past Kyle into the narrow corridor. The floor was packed dirt, and the walls were rough limestone. "Yes, this seems like..." I

began to say and then I stopped when I saw a slight,

illuminated figure hovering several yards ahead. My heart

leapt - it looked like Amanda Lee.

"Hello?" I called tentatively, stepping past Kyle

into the corridor. "Amanda Lee?"

"L.J., who do you see?" Van asked, following

behind me.

The figure wavered in front of me as if she was

undecided whether or not she should wait. I didn't want

to lose her. Not when we were so close.

Not stopping to answer Van, I hurried forward,

moving as quickly as I could on the uneven ground, my

heart pounding rapidly. "Amanda Lee, is that you?"

I was close enough now to see her. Well, actually,

see through her. It wasn't Amanda Lee – even in her

beyond-life state, I could see that this was a younger girl,

just in her teens. She was wearing a sequined party dress,

too old for her years, and her garish blood-red lipstick had

been smeared onto her cheeks.

"Honey?" I asked softly. "Honey, are you okay?"

She turned large blue eyes to me, filled with translucent tears. "Those men. Those men hurt me. They hurt me real bad," she whispered, her body shaking convulsively.

"Oh, sweetheart, I'm so sorry," I replied, my throat tight with emotion.

She took a deep breath and tried to smile. "But I got away," she said with pride. "After they put me in that dark place, I got away and hid here."

"That was so smart of you," I replied with encouragement, but a pit was growing in my stomach. "Do you remember where the dark place was?"

"It was by a big, old house," she said. "A scary place. But I got out of there quick as I could and hightailed it here."

The distance between the Old Crenshaw Place and Grammy Anderson's was at least ten miles. There was no way she..."

"Funny thing," she continued. "It didn't take me but a moment to get here. All I could think of was getting somewhere safe and then it was like magic."

"Magic," I whispered, my lips trembling as I accepted the terrible truth. "How long have you been hiding down here, honey?"

The girl slowly shook her head. "Not long," she insisted. "Not long at all."

"What's today's date?" I asked her.

"June 19th, 1995," she replied. "I just graduated from high school end of last month."

I gasped softly. She'd been down here for more than fifteen years. She'd been missing for more than fifteen years.

"I'm Louella Jo Carter," I said, trying to keep my voice even. "What's your name?"

"Pammy," she said. "Pammy Jo Weston."

Chapter Thirty-eight

We didn't have a lot of success at the speakeasy. Pammy Jo faded away moments after she revealed her name, so I couldn't get any more information about her and, although we spent another two hours turning the speakeasy inside and out, we never found anything resembling files connected to the Sons of the Mississippi. Or anyone else for that matter.

I was tired, frustrated, hungry, and I was wearing ugly boots.

"You hungry?" Van asked as we drove back home together.

"No," I lied.

He glanced over at me and smiled. "You are not a good liar," he said.

"Well, I am not as hungry as I am tired, and I am not as tired as I am frustrated," I explained. "And I am not as frustrated as I am totally embarrassed by my ugly footwear. So, we can't go get anything to eat."

His smile faded and he just stared at me for a long moment, then he shrugged and looked back down the road. I think he might have muttered something like, "Women." But I really can't be totally sure.

"How about a drive-thru," he finally suggested. "Pick up some burgers or tacos. No one will even see your feet if we drive-thru."

"It's late," I countered. "I think most of the drive-thrus are closed."

He glanced at the clock on the dashboard. "Okay, I know a place where your shoes won't matter," he said, turning right at the next intersection.

"Where?" I asked, with a little concern.

"It's a surprise."

I shook my head. "Really. I don't think I need any more surprises in my life if that's okay with you."

He turned once more, and I realized that we were on the pier. "What?"

"I've got some snapper I could grill," he said. "And the makings of a salad, if that's okay."

221

I instantly regretted being so surly, and I smiled at him. "That would be really nice," I replied. "Thank you."

He shrugged and pulled into the parking spot by his slip. He got out of the truck, then came around to my side and opened the door.

"And thank you for putting up with me," I said, slipping down into his arms.

This time he smiled and placed a quick kiss on my forehead. "You're welcome," he said, slipping his arm around my shoulders and guiding me toward the boat. "While I cook, why don't you take a nap on the bunk below deck. Then I'll call you when the food's ready."

I didn't even consider arguing, I was so tired. So, I gratefully headed below deck once we climbed onto the boat. Dusky light filtered in through the windows, giving everything a pinkish-orange hue. The narrow cot had crisp cotton sheets and a light throw and looked so inviting. I pulled off my ugly boots, lay down on the bed, and burrowed my head into the cool, softness of the pillow.

Even in the slip, there was a gentle movement on the boat, a calm lulling movement, like a rocking chair, and within moments I was sound asleep.

The soft whirl of dark colors against my eyelids slowly began to take shape. Suddenly I was back at the speakeasy, staring down the narrow corridor. The lighter limestone walls and the dark dirt path blended into each other, turning the corridor into a cave or a tunnel. I stepped forward and could feel the cool, hard-packed dirt beneath my bare feet.

There was no light, so I moved forward slowly, reaching out on either side of me to lightly touch the walls to maintain my balance. The smell of the swamp grew stronger as I continued forward; decaying vegetation, stagnant water, and rotting wood. I paused at one point to look behind me and discovered the way back was just as dark as the way forward.

"Hello?" I whispered, my throat dry and tight.

Finally, I could see a dim light at the end of the tunnel. I jogged ahead, the ground beneath me changing from hard-packed dirt, to loose soil, and finally, to mud, squishing between my toes as I ran.

"Hello!" I called out, my voice a little stronger.

The light was still there.

I ran faster, even as the mud deepened, and tried to enclose my feet. Suddenly the walls were no longer around me and I was running through a swamp. Spanish moss hanging from old, thick Cypress trees swept over my skin like a shroud. I shivered and batted it away as I increased my pace toward the light.

Finally, I could see a waterway. The ground beneath my feet became more solid and a boat slowly made its way up the channel to stop right in front of me. I could see now that the light had been from the ship's window. Something below deck must be illuminated and was glowing in the dark. I stepped onto the deck and hurried toward the window with eager anticipation.

A face, pale and drawn, appeared in the window. Dark, scraggly hair tumbled across a bloated and lifeless face. JoEllen. JoEllen was on the boat. I screamed and jumped back.

"Help me," she whispered, as water poured from her mouth.

I turned away, only to be confronted by another woman. Her face was bruised and swollen. Her head was tilted to the side and there was a large red abrasion around her neck.

"Louella Jo," she said, smiling with unseeing eyes. "How nice of you to join us."

Amanda Lee. It was Amanda Lee.

I stepped back, toward the edge of the deck.

"No," I cried. "No, I don't want to join you."

"Why not?" asked a voice to my side. I turned and realized that now JoEllen was coming up on the other side of me. "You too good for us?"

I shook my head. "I'm trying…I'm trying to help you," I cried. "Please, I'm trying…"

"How you gonna help us if we're dead?" Amanda Lee shouted. "Unless you want to keep us company."

I stepped back and found myself trapped against the side of the boat, Amanda Lee on one side only a few feet away, and JoEllen on the other, slowly closing the distance between us.

I looked over my shoulder and now the water was sloshing up against the side, dark and deadly. I realized that if I jumped, I would be joining them.

"No, please," I sobbed. "Please. Please, I just want to help you."

They both laughed mirthlessly and, with arms outstretched moved towards me.

"Nooooo!"

Chapter Thirty-nine

"L.J.! L.J., sweetheart. Wake up!"

I could hear Van's voice trying to pull me out of the depths of my dream.

"No," I cried, fighting my way back. "No, please."

Then, suddenly, I was awake.

I sprang up into a sitting position; my heart pounding, my breathing labored, and tears pouring down my face. Then I was gathered into a strong, safe embrace and I let the terror ebb. I laid my head against his chest and took deep cleansing breaths until the shuddering stopped. Finally, when my heart had calmed and my mind had cleared, I became aware that Van was rubbing my back with gentle movements and whispering soothing words in my ear.

"It's okay, sweetheart," he murmured. "You're safe. Nothing is going to hurt you. I'll protect you."

My heart melted a little and I sat up and met his eyes.

"I'm better," I said, inhaling deeply. "Much better. Thanks."

"What happened?" he asked immediately, then paused and shook his head. "No. Don't tell me if it's too upsetting."

"I'm fine," I replied. "It was a dream. A really bad dream. A really realistic bad dream featuring dead people who wanted to kill me."

I shuddered involuntarily and Van drew me into his arms again. "I'm so sorry," he began, then he stopped and sniffed the air.

I smelled it too.

There's nothing worse than the smell of burning fish on a grill.

"Damn," he said softly, and I admired his control. "I forgot all about them."

"Thank you," I replied, leaning forward, and kissing him.

228

He smiled down at me and gently stroked my cheek. "I guess I'm not very good at multi-tasking," he said.

"Well, I have eggs at my place," I offered. "We could have scrambled eggs and toast."

His smile widened. "Sounds perfect," he said. "Let me turn off the grill and close the lid. I'll do clean up in the morning."

Chapter Forty

"Where have you two kids been?" Kyle asked as we walked into the house fifteen minutes later. "I'm making omelets. Are you hungry?"

Van winked at me and laughed.

"Starving," I replied. "Thanks for asking."

"I tried cooking for her," Van added. "But I had no idea she didn't like blackened fish."

I snorted, then clapped my hand over my mouth. "Not fair," I laughed, and we followed Kyle back into the kitchen.

The omelets were delicious and hit the spot. But as soon as I'd eaten, I couldn't seem to keep my eyes open. I'm sure I nodded off at the table at least once.

"Go to bed," Van ordered after I'd nearly face-planted on the table.

"What?" I asked drowsily.

"Go upstairs and go to bed," he said.

I yawned widely and nodded. "Yeah, good idea," I replied, pushing my chair back and slowly standing up.

I gave Kyle a hug. "Thanks for dinner," I said. "It was amazing."

"You're welcome," he said, hugging me back. "Now get some sleep."

"I'm on my way," I turned around and found Van in my path.

He pulled me gently into his arms and kissed me until my lips were throbbing and my knees were melting. "What was that for?" I asked, bemused.

"To ensure you have pleasant dreams," he said, bending and placing a gentler kiss on my lips. "Sweet dreams, L.J."

I sighed and nodded. "Yeah. Right. Thanks," I said, still muddled from the kiss. "Sweet dreams."

I made my way upstairs and to my bedroom, washed up quickly, and slid between the sheets in record time. I could still feel the pressure of Van's lips on mine and I fell asleep with a smile on my face.

231

My bliss didn't last very long. Two hours later, I woke up in a cold sweat, having dreamt about Amanda Lee and JoEllen once again.

I tossed the sheet to the side and slipped out of bed, walking to the bathroom to splash cold water on my face. When I lifted my head and glanced in the mirror, I gasped to see a face behind me in the bathroom.

"Momma!" I scolded, spinning around. "Don't ever do that to me again!"

"What?" Momma asked, perplexed. "What did I do?"

"You snuck up on me! You appeared out of nowhere," I accused.

Momma put her hands on her hips and slowly shook her head. "As you have been so eager to point out lately, I'm dead," she replied. "I can't help but appear out of nowhere and sneak up on folks."

I leaned against the sink and nodded, while my poor heart tried once again to regain its normal rate.

"You're right," I admitted. "I'm sorry. I just had another bad dream, and I don't think I can take one more scare."

"You want me to sit in the rocking chair and watch over you?" she offered, gently stroking my forehead. The coolness of her touch was welcome on my hot face.

"That'd be nice," I said. "Real nice."

"Well, come on then, back to bed with you," she urged.

Feeling like a ten-year-old, I hurried back to my bed, slipped under the covers, and closed my eyes. I could hear the soft creak of the old rocking chair and it seemed like my heart fell into rhythm with the sound. How many times in my life had Momma sat there, watching over me while I slept? How many times did she chase all the monsters and the disappointments away, by just being there?

"I love you, Momma," I whispered.

"I love you too, Sweetpea," she replied. "Now you go on and sleep."

I closed my eyes and tried drifting off, but that didn't work. I turned my pillow over and tried the other side, but that didn't work. I turned, so I was facing the other way, but that didn't work. Finally, in frustration, I sat up and looked across the room at my momma. "I can't fall asleep," I sighed.

"Well, maybe you just need something to take your mind off your dreams," she suggested. She glided over to my dresser. "Maybe something to read."

She lifted up the old portfolio that I'd found in the Crenshaw House. "How about this?" she asked, carrying it over to me.

I clicked on the bedside lamp and took the old book. "Sure, it's just a bunch of names," I said. "It's sure to put me to sleep."

I opened the book and began to read down the list of names. "Okay, not surprising," I said, seeing the names of Deputy Hill, Harold Murphy, Congressman Patterson, and a few other members of the Chamber of Commerce who I had suspected were involved.

234

I yawned. Momma was right, this was the perfect book for putting myself to sleep.

Flipping the page, I started reading the next entries. Yep. Yep. Yep. They all made sense.

Then I saw a name that made my jaw drop.

"That can't be right," I exclaimed softly. "No, that just can't be right."

"Who?" Momma asked. "Whose name is in there?"

I looked up at Momma, a pit in my stomach the size of a watermelon, and felt the anger and disappointment grow in my chest.

"Clarence Budington Featherstone," I whispered sadly. "Bud."

Chapter Forty-one

I didn't sleep very well after discovering Bud's name on the list of the members of the Sons of Mississippi. I kept debating whether or not I should tell Kyle what I found. I finally decided I had to tell him. He would be hurt, but at least he would know the truth.

"You're lying," Kyle exclaimed the next morning after I told him what I'd found.

"Why would I lie about this?" I asked.

Kyle threw his hands up in the air and marched around the table. "I have no idea," he said. "All I know is that you are lying. There is no way Bud would be involved in a group like the Sons of Mississippi."

"So, you think someone else signed his name in the book?" I asked, incredulously.

Kyle paused for a moment and then nodded. "Yes. Yes, that's it," he said firmly. "That has to be it. Someone wanted to frame him. Someone wanted to make him look bad."

I pulled out the contract Bud had signed once I gave him the dollar bill to represent me and shoved them towards Kyle. "The signatures match, Kyle," I said. "They completely match. Bud signed both of these."

Kyle refused to look at the paper and just shook his head. "You know what your problem is?" he asked angrily.

"No, Kyle, what's my problem?" I challenged.

"You don't understand what it is to have a real relationship with someone. In a real relationship you trust someone first," he shouted. "You don't immediately think the worst of them."

"I didn't immediately think the worst of him. I have always admired Bud. But this," I yelled back, shaking the papers in front of him. "This is irrefutable evidence. You can't just turn a blind eye to this and pretend it's not real."

Kyle shook his head. "Oh, yes, I can," he said. Then he marched past me, down the hall, and out the door, slamming it behind him.

237

"Ouch," Momma said, appearing next to me. "That didn't go well at all."

I slunk into the nearest seat. "Tell me about it," I sighed, dropping the portfolio and contract on the kitchen table. "I thought I was being helpful."

Momma sat down across from me. "You were," she said. "You were being helpful. You just weren't being kind."

"What?" I stammered. I couldn't believe my own mother just said that. "What did you just say?"

"Don't take that tone with me, young lady," Momma immediately reprimanded me. "I know you. Maybe even better than you know yourself."

This was just ridiculous! I was up all night trying to figure out what to do, I did what I thought was best. She just needed to understand it from my perspective.

"Wait. I find out that Bud's name is on the portfolio. I know that Kyle is in a relationship with Bud. Kyle is my friend, so I tell him what I found out, so he's protected."

238

"And you're the hero," Momma added quietly.

"What?" I gasped angrily. Is she kidding me?

"And you're the hero," she repeated.

I pushed away from the table and started to stand up.

"You sit your butt straight back down, young lady," Momma ordered.

Years of training had me obeying, but not liking it. "What?" I asked, my voice clipped and surly.

"I didn't mean to hurt your feelings," Momma said.

"Well, you did," I grumbled.

"Okay, think about this for a minute," she said, her voice surprisingly calm. "What choices did you have this morning."

"What do you mean?"

"What choices did you have this morning?" she repeated. "Obviously choice number one was to tell Kyle all about what you found."

I nodded. "Which I did," I said.

239

"Choice number two?" Momma asked.

I shrugged impatiently. "Well, I could have compared his signature to another one of his signatures to make sure they matched," I snipped. "Oh, wait, I did that."

So there, Momma, I thought triumphantly.

"You could have gone to Bud and asked him why his name was in the portfolio," she said.

Wait, this was not going the way I thought it would.

"Yeah," I agreed. "I guess I could have done that."

"And then, if there was something wrong, you could have asked Bud to go to Kyle and explain everything," she continued. "So, he could do it in his own way. But, instead, you wanted to save Kyle. You wanted to fix things. You wanted to…"

Crap.

"Be the hero," I admitted softly. Then I shook my head. "But I didn't mean to… That wasn't my intent… I just was trying…"

"To help your friend," Momma finished. "Yeah, I know. Been there, done that. Which is the only reason I'm mentioning it now. I've been the 'helpful' friend and then I discovered I really wasn't all that helpful after all."

"But your heart was in the right place, wasn't it?" I asked, more for myself than Momma.

"If roles were reversed. If Kyle discovered something about Van. Would you have preferred to have him go to Van first and allow Van to explain things to you or go to you?" she asked me.

"Come to me," I said. "I'd want to…"

Momma chuckled. "Okay, change that. If Kyle found out something about you, would you prefer he come to you first or go to Van?"

Well, that made a world of difference.

I sighed. "Yeah, you're right, I'd want him to come to me, so at least I could explain myself."

"There could be an explanation for Bud's name being on that list," Momma said. "I've known him for a long time and I'm usually a fairly good judge of people."

"Yeah, but..."

"But lately you don't know who you can trust, right?"

"Right," I agreed with a nod. "But what I did to Kyle wasn't fair."

Momma lifted her eyebrow. You know, one of those momma looks that says a lot more than words.

"And it wasn't fair to Bud either," I added.

I stood up and slipped my purse over my shoulder. "I guess I better get going," I said with a resigned shrug. "I'm going to have Ida cancel my morning appointments, so I can get over to Bud's and talk to him."

"That's my girl," Momma said.

"Thanks, Momma," I replied, and I wondered if I would ever be old enough not to need my mother's advice. I shook my head.

Probably not.

Chapter Forty-two

It was still early in the morning when I got to Bud's farm. I slipped off my high heels and slipped on the ugly boots before I got out of my car. The ground between the parking area and the barn was hard-packed and dry, but I knew that once I entered the dairy barn, all bets were off.

I took a deep breath, inhaling the sweet scent of freshly mowed hay mixed with the earthly smell of fresh manure. It wasn't a totally unpleasant smell, just a scent unique to barns and rural America.

The barn door was open, so I slipped inside. Bud was standing in the middle of the milking parlor wearing overalls and a tall pair of rubber boots. He had a shovel in his hands and was scooping a steaming pile of manure up from the concrete barn floor and sliding it into the grate-covered gutter. The cows around him munched contentedly on grain, while the electric milkers pumped the milk from their udders through a vacuum system of

243

clear plastic pipes to a refrigerated holding tank in a separate room.

Bud put down the shovel and stepped forward to remove the milkers from a cow and then opened a gate, so she could walk out of the barn, back to the pasture. Another cow slowly ambled forward, ready to take her place.

Bud reached in and wiped the cow's udders, then placed the milkers on her teats, while the cow maneuvered her head into the grain bin and helped herself. A moment later, milk was streaming up through the pipes into the system.

I stepped up and tapped Bud on the shoulder. He initially started in response, turning quickly and defensively, then I saw him contain himself and calm down.

"Sorry," he said, raising his voice to be heard over the machinery and the bellowing. "I'm not used to having anyone come up behind me."

"I should apologize," I said. "I guess I should have knocked or something."

"Come into the tank room," he said, motioning to a door at the end of the milking parlor. "We can talk without shouting in there."

I followed him down the line and into a large room where large stainless milk coolers thrummed softly as milk poured into them through the clear tubes. Once Bud closed the door it was much quieter.

"This is better," I agreed.

He smiled and nodded. "So, what can I do for you?" he asked.

"I don't remember if I told you about the portfolio I found at the Crenshaw house," I began, intently watching for any reaction.

He thought about it for a moment, then shook his head. "You told me so much about what had happened to you," he said. "I don't know if I remember either, but I'm sure if you did, I have it in my notes."

I didn't notice any hesitancy on his part. So, I figured I'd just continue.

"Well, last night I ended up looking through the portfolio," I explained. "I saw a bunch of names I figured would be on the list. And then…"

There it was. Fear.

"I saw your name," I finished.

He nodded slowly and exhaled softly. "I'm sorry," he said. "I'm sorry you had to see that."

My mind raced and my heart thumped against my chest. Isn't that what people say just before they kill someone and bury them in the back forty?

"I don't understand," I finally replied.

"When I did that…when I joined them…I was a very confused young man," he said. "I knew I wasn't satisfied with my life. I knew that something was missing. I knew that I wanted to feel like a part of something."

Pulling off his gloves, he reached into his pocket for a handkerchief and wiped the perspiration from his brow.

246

"Back then. Back when I joined them," he said, "Being a gay man in the South just wasn't acceptable. So, you hid who you were. You hid your feelings. And you tried, as hard as hell, to fit in with the "normal" guys."

He stuffed the handkerchief back into his pocket. "That's what the Sons of Mississippi were to me," he said. "They were the good old boys. They were the pillars of the community. They were the men who pulled the strings and if you got in with them, your business was secure."

Shaking his head, he leaned against one of the coolers. "I went to the Old Crenshaw Place for some kind of ceremony," he said. "Patterson himself invited me. Told me they could use a smart young lawyer on the team. Didn't even have to pass any kind of initiation. He'd vouch for me. He knew my family."

Laughing bitterly, he slapped his gloves against his leg. "He knew my family," he said with some disgust. "What he meant was that he knew my daddy was a bigot and a bully and figured I'd fit the same mold."

He sighed.

247

"Anyway, it stormed that day, a bad storm, so we didn't have whatever outside ceremony they'd planned. Then a couple of weeks later, I went to their first meeting, and I realized who they were," he said, looking up and meeting my eyes. "I was sick to my stomach. I was disgusted that I allowed myself to even associate with them. I got up, walked out, and never went back."

"You should have told me."

"Kyle," I gasped, turning to see him standing at the door.

But he wasn't looking at me, he was looking directly at Bud.

Bud nodded. "Yes, you're right," he agreed. "I should have told you. Especially once you told me about your involvement with the Sons of Mississippi."

"Why didn't you?" Kyle asked, his voice cool and angry.

"I was ashamed," Bud admitted. "I didn't want you to know. You have to believe me; I am not the same man I was when I joined that group."

248

"I really want to believe you," Kyle said with more hurt than anger.

I looked at both men, Bud's eyes pleading for forgiveness and Kyle's eyes filled with pain and doubt. This was something they needed to work out without me, I would only be in the way.

"I'm going to leave," I said, slipping through the door. "So, you two can talk."

Neither said a word. I don't know if either of them even heard what I said because they were so focused on each other.

I softly closed the door behind me and hurried to my car and prayed that they would be able to work it out.

Chapter Forty-three

When Ida locked the door after the final customer left the salon, I wanted to cry out in a loud voice, "Hallelujah!" Instead, I just collapsed into my chair and closed my eyes in relief.

"Tough day boss," Maribelle said, handing me a cold can of diet soda. "You deserve a cold one."

I opened my eyes, pulled the tab, and took a long, satisfying drink. "Thank you," I sighed. "I'm so glad this day is over."

"I can't believe you took both your customers and Kyle's customers," Ida said, scooting into a chair near mine.

"Well, it was the least I could do," I said, then I took another sip. "After all, if I handled things better…"

"You were just looking out for him," Kasey said, leaning against the counter and eating a candy bar. "He's, you know, family."

I nodded. "Yeah, but I should have gone to Bud in the first place," I replied. "I mean, once he told me what had happened, I totally understood."

"So, did they make up?" Georgia asked as she massaged her foot from her chair.

I grinned. "Well, all I know is that they decided to take a drive to New Orleans, and I shouldn't expect him back early," I said. "So, yeah, I'm thinking they made up."

"So, they won't be going back to the diner tonight, will they?" Ida asked.

I shook my head. "Afraid not," I said. "And we didn't find anything yesterday when we searched."

"You think those Sons of Mississippi going to give you a lot more chances to look?" Maribelle asked.

"I don't know," I said with a shrug. "I mean, there's nothing I can do about it…"

"I have a key," Ida exclaimed.

"What?" Georgia asked.

"Grammy gave it to my momma, cause momma used to help at the diner sometimes," she replied.

251

"You have a key to the diner?" I asked.

"And the house," Ida said. "I searched for them last night and found them. I knew I had them somewhere."

"I'm thinking a bunch of women could do a much better job searching for something another woman hid than a bunch of men," Maribelle said.

"Ohhhh! I want in," Kasey said. "I just need to make a call…"

"Buddy's home tonight," Georgia added. "I'll just let him know I have to work late."

Okay, this is getting out of hand.

"No," I said, shaking my head. "This could be dangerous. I can't let…"

"Ida, did you come by those keys legally?" Maribelle asked, cutting me off.

"I sure did," Ida said. "They were given to us in case we needed to get in the house or the diner. No conditions."

Maribelle turned to me and shrugged. "I guess we're all going to help Ida look through her second cousin's place tonight," she announced.

"Third cousin twice-removed," Ida corrected.

"Right," Maribelle said with a quick nod, then she turned back to me. "Want to come?"

Chapter Forty-four

"This is so much fun!" Ida squealed as they walked down the overgrown path toward the house. Her flashlight beam bobbing all over the place.

"Shhhhhh!" Georgia said, walking right behind her. "Someone might hear you?"

"Who?" Maribelle asked casually. "An alligator?"

"There's alligators out here?" Kasey exclaimed, shining her flashlight into the brush. "Why didn't anyone tell me?"

I stood behind the group and muffled a chuckle. Well, if nothing else, this is certainly going to be an experience I'll never forget.

Ida climbed the shaky steps to the rotted porch. "It's a lot worse than I remember," she said, hesitant to step forward.

"When was the last time you were here?" Georgia asked.

Ida paused for a moment to think. "Must have been when I was about thirteen," she replied slowly.

"You haven't been here for over forty years, and you're surprised it's changed?" Georgia asked.

"Well, you know, it didn't seem that long ago until you mentioned it," Ida replied. She tentatively put one foot forward to test the floorboards and moved forward as she found solid support ahead. It took her several minutes, but she finally made it to the doorway, inserted the key, and pushed the door open.

"Well, it still works," she said, pleased with herself.

"You weren't sure it worked?" Kasey asked, slowly stepping up the rickety stairs as she continued to search the brush for alligators with her flashlight beam.

"Well, it has been forty years," Ida replied defensively.

"There's a light switch on the right," I called, eager to get inside and away from the mosquitos and other creatures of the swamp.

255

I saw the house glow with light and breathed a sigh of relief. Okay, we're in. Now the real fun begins.

I was the last to enter the house and the last to be given a pair of black plastic gloves by Maribelle. "What are these for?" I asked as I slipped them on.

"You don't want to leave any fingerprints or DNA evidence laying around," she replied, as she sat on the arm of the couch. "I'm surprised you didn't think of these."

Me too, I thought.

"So, where do you think we should search?" Ida asked me.

I shrugged. "Well, you knew Grammy Anderson better than all of us," I said. "Where do you think she'd hide those files?"

"If it was me, I'd hide them in my house," Georgia said. "Folks would think to look in the speakeasy, but they probably wouldn't think of looking here at the house."

"Well, we didn't have any luck when we searched the speakeasy," I replied. "So, that makes just about as much sense as anything else."

"Let's divide and conquer," Maribelle suggested. "Ida, you and Georgia search the kitchen."

"Wait!" Ida exclaimed. "I have a better idea."

This is not going to be good, I decided.

"I saw this on a made-for-tv movie," Ida continued, waving her hands with excitement. "These folks were trying to find out where this dead person buried this expensive necklace..."

"How did she bury a necklace if she was dead?" Kasey asked, screwing up her face in confusion.

"No. She buried the necklace just before she died," Ida explained.

"Why?" Kasey asked. "You can't wear it if it's got dirt all over it."

"Because she knew someone was going to kill her," Ida replied.

"Well, then why did she take the time to bury a necklace, she should have been going to the police," Kasey said, shaking her head. "What? Was she crazy or something?"

Ida nodded eagerly. "Well, actually, she was going to call the police, but then the phone lines all went dead, and she was living in this old mansion, and all the servants were out for the night. And then, she heard the door open, and she knew…"

"Can you just cut to the point?" Maribelle interrupted. "What's your better idea?"

"A séance!" Ida exclaimed.

"No," the rest of us immediately responded.

"Why not?" Ida asked, crestfallen. "It's a great idea."

Georgia shook her head. "Oh, no, I've seen too many of those movies where they have a séance for fun and then accidentally release a demon," she said. "And then it follows them home. I have enough to do with Buddy and the kids, I don't need no demon in my house."

258

"But it won't be a demon," Ida pleaded. "It will be Grammy Anderson."

"Can you guarantee that?" Maribelle asked. "Can you guarantee that no one else will answer your summoning?"

"See, what you just said there, summoning. I'm sure that's the name of one of those movies," Georgia said, shivering slightly and rubbing her arms. "That's a sign. That's a sure sign we shouldn't be doing that."

Ida looked so sad that I had to offer her some consolation. "Well, since you were related to her," I said. "Why don't you just try to reach out to Grammy, without the whole séance thing. Just talk to her and see if she comes to you."

Ida brightened. "Do you think that would work?"

I shrugged. "Well, I don't think it would hurt."

"Okay," Ida said. "I'll go to the kitchen and get started."

Maribelle stood up and rolled her eyes. "Okay, the rest of us should split up and start searching everywhere else. If you find something, call for backup."

"Call for backup?" I whispered to Maribelle, biting back a smile.

Maribelle chuckled softly. "Ida's not the only one who watches tv."

Chapter Forty-five

Everyone scattered to different parts of the house, and I followed Ida into the kitchen. The room was a mess, courtesy of Grammy's grandsons, but Ida was able to find a semi-clean chair pulled up next to the kitchen table. I stood in the doorway, on the other side of the room, giving Ida plenty of space to perform whatever ritual she thought would work.

Ida sat her plump body on the chair, rested her hands on her knees, and touched her thumbs to her middle fingers as if she was meditating. Then she closed her eyes and started to rock slowly back and forth.

"Grammy Anderson," she called out, her voice much lower than usual and slightly musical. "Grammy Anderson, I beseech you to appear to me."

"What the hell is that girl doing?" Grammy Anderson asked when she appeared next to me.

"She's summoning you," I whispered.

"Grammy Anderson," Ida repeated, her voice a little louder.

"Does she think I'm deaf?" Grammy asked.

I bit back a giggle. "Well, she probably doesn't realize how close you are," I replied softly.

"Grammy Anderson. We need your help," Ida chanted loudly.

"Oh, she needs help all right," Grammy said, staring at her relative. "Serious help." Then she turned to me. "What's this all about?"

"We're trying to find your files," I whispered. "The ones on the Sons of Mississippi."

"I told you already, you'll be cooking up nothing but trouble with those files," she said.

I stepped out of the kitchen, into the empty hallway and Grammy followed me.

"Did you know Pammy Jo Weston?" I asked quietly.

Grammy nodded. "Yes, sweetest little thing," she said with a smile. "She up and disappeared just after she graduated from high school. They said they saw her working in New Orleans. I guess the city life was more her style."

"They lied to you. They killed her."

"What?" Grammy asked, shaking her head in disbelief. "No. No, they wouldn't have…"

"I met her ghost in the passageway from the speakeasy to the swamp," I said, my voice shaking with quiet anger. "She thought she was safe there. She thought she'd escaped from them after they hurt her. She thought she'd been able to get out of the dark place and come for help. But what she didn't know, doesn't know, is that only her spirit escaped. Her body is still hidden somewhere, in some dark place, where they dumped her after they abused her."

Grammy continued to shake her head. "No," she whispered. "They wouldn't…they couldn't…"

"Come on," I replied, meeting her eyes. "You knew who they were. You didn't trust them. Or you wouldn't have kept notes on them for your own safety.

263

You can't tell me that you didn't worry that something bad had happened to Pammy Jo."

Grammy was silent for a long moment, then she trembled and nodded. "I confess, I did worry when she turned up missing," she admitted sadly, her eyes downcast. "I worried that they'd taken her. But then, when I heard…"

"You still doubted it, didn't you?" I challenged her. "But you turned a blind eye to it."

She looked up at me, her eyes filled with regret. "I did," she whispered despondently. "God forgive me, I did."

Then she disappeared.

Okay, so maybe I pushed her a little too far.

I walked back into the kitchen, surprised to find the chair Ida had been occupying empty and the room deserted. "Ida?" I called, more than a little concerned. "Ida, where are you?"

"Now you're sounding like me," Ida laughed as she stepped out of the pantry. "But you need to lower your voice and make it like a chant." Then she demonstrated. "Ida. Ida. We need you."

I laughed, walked over to her, and gave her a hug. "Yes, we do," I said. "We definitely need you. So, how did it go? Did you reach Grammy Anderson?"

She shook her head. "No, but I found something even better," she replied.

"The files?" I asked eagerly.

She shook her head and her excitement disappeared. "Sorry, no," she apologized. "I found Grammy's recipe box. I've always wanted…"

She met my eyes. "This belongs to the boys, doesn't it?"

"Like they are ever going to use it," I replied. "Why don't you take it and I'll ask Bud to ask the boys for you."

Her smile lit up the entire room as she hugged the metal card file to her bosom. "Thank you so much," she said. "I can't wait to start…"

She stopped and sniffed. "Do you smell…"

"Fire!" Maribelle screamed, running into the kitchen. "The whole damn house is on fire!"

Chapter Forty-six

I really wanted to panic. Panic actually seemed like the best possible choice in this scenario. But I was responsible for these women, and I didn't have the time or the luxury to panic.

"Where is everyone else?" I asked Maribelle.

"In the living room," she said, coughing as the air filled with smoke.

"Let's go," I replied, grabbing Ida's arm and pulling her with me into the living room.

Once there, I saw Kasey and Georgia at the door. Georgia turned to me, her face filled with fear. "It's jammed shut," she cried. "Someone locked us in."

Don't panic. Don't panic. Don't panic.

"Okay, the windows are boarded up," I said, looking around the room. "The front door is locked. So, we go out the back door."

As we turned to run into the kitchen the lights went out.

Someone screamed. I think it was Kasey.

"Turn on your flashlights," I yelled. "Into the kitchen."

I hurried forward, back into the kitchen. The smoke was getting pretty thick, but I remembered there was a mudroom at the back of the house. "This way," I called.

I hurried through the kitchen, found the doorway, and tripped down the step. "There's a step," I yelled. "At the door, there's a step-down."

As the ladies followed me, I took a moment to look around the room. The back door was boarded up too, but next to it was an old ax, probably for splitting wood.

"Georgia," I called as I ran across the room. "Call 911 and get the Fire Department here."

I picked up the ax and swung with all my might. A tiny crack appeared in the wood. It looked a lot easier when they did it on tv.

Maribelle came up behind me. "Give it to me," she said.

Without argument, I handed her the ax and stepped back. She hefted the ax and swung with all of her might. The door hinge gave away and the door swung partially away from the frame. It wasn't a big opening, but it was an opening.

"Georgia, Kasey, Maribelle, out, out, out," I ordered.

"Georgia and Kasey go," Maribelle said. "I want to give this sucker another crack."

Georgia and Kasey pushed themselves out of the small opening, gasping for air.

"Ida," I called. "Ida, we're next."

But Ida didn't respond.

"Ida?" I screamed, shining my flashlight beam into the smoky room. "Ida, where are you?"

"I thought she was right behind us," Maribelle exclaimed.

"Keep hitting that door," I told her. "I'll find her."

I moved back through the smoke, retracing my steps into the kitchen. "Ida," I called.

"Oh, help," Ida called out. "I lost my flashlight. I can't see anything."

I moved forward, pulling my shirt up over my mouth and nose in order to breathe. "Where are you?" I coughed.

"The pantry," she cried out.

I turned toward the small room and could make out Ida's figure in the doorway. "I'm here…" I said, reaching for her.

Suddenly, the small pantry exploded into flames. I grabbed Ida's arm and yanked her forward. She stumbled against me and nearly took us both down. I looped her arm over my shoulder and half-dragged her through the kitchen to the mudroom.

"Almost there," I gasped.

"One more hit," Maribelle yelled.

I heard the crash, felt the influx of fresh air, and then my whole world exploded.

Chapter Forty-seven

"Honey. Honey, can you hear me?"

I opened my eyes slowly, the room was bright, too bright. "Momma?" I called out.

"Oh, honey, your momma isn't here."

I looked over to where the second voice was coming from, and a white-clad nurse stood next to my bed. Then I looked on the other side of the bed and saw Momma standing there, her face filled with fear.

"Momma?" I whispered, still a little dazed.

"Hush now, Louella Jo," Momma said. "This here nurse has no idea that I'm a ghost. And if you keep on talking to me, they're going to keep you here for a psychological examination."

Right. That's right. She's dead.

I turned back to the nurse. "Where am I?"

"You're at the hospital," she said. "You were in a house fire."

Suddenly I remembered and tried to sit up. "Ida. Where's Ida?" I cried.

The nurse, who was surprisingly strong, pushed me gently back into a prone position. "Now you just lay there for a moment," she said. "And I'll give you all the information you need to know."

Fair enough. I can lay quiet for a minute.

"Ida is down the hall in another room," she said. "From what the Fire Chief said, as soon as the fresh air hit the fire, it caused some kind of fireball that exploded behind you. You and Ida got hit from behind with fiery debris, but somehow, you still managed to pull her out of the house. She took the brunt of the explosion because she was behind you. But you got pretty beat up yourself."

"Is she going to be okay?"

The look in the nurse's eyes belied the comforting words of encouragement that were coming from her mouth. "I'm sure she will be fine," she assured me.

I smiled and nodded; my throat too tight to say anything.

272

"You've got someone who's been wanting to see you," she continued, eager to change the subject. "Are you up to company?"

I nodded again. Whoever it was would be able to give me good information about Ida.

I heard the nurse's soft-soled shoes squeak across the room, heard the door open, and heard her whispered instructions. "Don't overdo it. She's obviously had enough trauma, poor dear. Talking to her dead momma like that."

The door closed again, and I heard heavier footsteps cross the room, then Van's worried face was peering over the side of the bed. "Hey," he said softly, as he gently stroked my cheek. "How are you doing?"

"I have no idea," I answered honestly. "They have me so strapped down; I can't move."

"You have a concussion," he said. "A piece of two-by-four caught you in the back of the head."

"That's it?" I asked. "Why can't I get up then?"

"Because you've been talking to your dead momma like she's standing in the room," he replied with a twinkle in his eye.

I turned to Momma, and I give her credit for looking a little embarrassed. "I'm sorry. But I was worried about you, so I asked you some questions," she admitted.

"And I answered them," I replied.

"Well, you did as you came in and out of consciousness," she said. "And you also inhaled a lot of smoke."

"Yeah, my throat feels raw," I replied. Then I looked directly into Van's eyes. "How is Ida."

He looked right back at me, not evading in the least. "It's gonna be touch and go for the next few hours," he said. "She inhaled a lot of smoke, and she got hit with a beam across her head and back. She's got some second-degree burns on her arms and back. They've done everything they can up to this point. Now they've got her on oxygen and are just monitoring her vitals."

"They did this to us," I said.

274

"What?" he asked urgently. "What do you mean?"

"Ida had a key," I explained. "So, we decided to check out the house for the files. Someone locked us in, barricaded the door, and started the fire."

"You mean they tried to kill you?" Momma exclaimed. "Kill all of you?"

"There was a car parked in front of the house," I said. "We had the lights on. There is no way they didn't know someone was in there."

"How many cars?" Van asked.

"One," I said. "We all got into my car."

"So, if they didn't see you all go in, they could have just assumed it was you, right?"

I nodded slowly. "So, it's my fault," I said softly.

"No, dammit!" Van growled. "It's not your fault. It's them. It's their fault."

He took a deep breath and slowly exhaled. "Maribelle told me that she was the one to smell the smoke," he said.

"Yeah, Ida and I were in the kitchen, and we weren't paying attention…"

"And Maribelle told me that she used the ax to cut down the door," he continued.

I nodded. "Yeah, remind me never to arm wrestle…"

"And if she hadn't been there. If you had been on your own…"

I gasped softly, remembering how ineffectual I'd been using that ax. "I'd be dead."

Chapter Forty-eight

It was a conspiracy.

A total conspiracy.

I was fine. I was totally fine.

And all I really wanted to do was go home and sleep in my own bed.

I mean, really, I'd been beaten up, shot at, attacked by a demon, chipped a nail on my luggage – a concussion is no big deal.

But I was overruled not only by the doctor, the nurses, but also Van, Momma, Georgia, Kasey, and Maribelle. I thought they were supposed to be on my side.

But at the end of visiting hours, they all waved goodbye, well, everyone but the doctor and nurses, and left me alone with my thoughts.

They weren't good thoughts. Since I couldn't see Ida, I had to assume the worst, right?

And assuming the worst made me angry – really angry.

And guilty – incredibly guilty.

She wouldn't have been there if it hadn't been for me. If I hadn't decided to let the ladies in on my secrets, Ida would have been home tonight, eating popcorn and watching some awful made-for-television movie. She would have been safe and happy.

"You're gonna get wrinkles if you keep screwing up your face like that," Momma said, appearing next to me.

"I don't care," I grumbled.

"You're not pouting about having to stay overnight in the hospital, are you?" Momma asked in a disappointed tone.

I sighed and shook my head. "Ouch," I replied as soon as I realized that my head still hurt. A lot. "I'm upset about Ida. I'm angry that this happened to her, and I feel responsible."

"Did you start the fire?" Momma shot back.

"Yeah, good try, but that's not going to work this time," I said. "She would not have been there if I hadn't told her, told all of them, about my secret."

"Well, that's one way to look at it," Momma said easily.

She didn't fool me.

"What other way is there to look at it, Momma?" I asked.

"Well, Ida did have a key to the house, right?"

I shrugged.

"And Ida would have found out about the boys being in jail, right?"

I nodded.

"Was there anything in that house that Ida might have wanted to…let's just say liberate?" Momma asked.

"Well, she was pretty happy at finding Grammy Anderson's recipe box," I said.

Maribelle actually told me that Ida held onto the box throughout the ride to the hospital and they had to pry it from her hands once they wheeled her into the

Emergency Room. But I wasn't going to tell that to Momma.

"But that doesn't mean she would have let herself into the house to take it."

"She might have," Momma said. "And she might have been alone in there when they started the fire."

"You can't say that Momma," I said. "You don't know."

"And you don't know either," she replied. "But, bottom line, we can't change the past, we can only go forward. So, what are you gonna do about it?"

What was I going to do about it?

My head ached, my body hurt, and I have to admit, I was a little scared.

"I don't know, Momma," I whispered, more tired than I cared to admit.

She reached over and I felt the coolness of her lips on my forehead. "Sleep on it, sweetheart," she advised. "Things always look clearer in the morning."

"Always?" I asked skeptically.

She chuckled softly. "Well, if they don't, at least you're not as tired when you're dealing with them."

I yawned and closed my eyes. "Will you stay?" I mumbled wearily.

"Of course, sweetheart," she replied gently. "Forever if I can."

Chapter Forty-nine

I woke up to find sunlight streaming through the hospital windows, my headache mostly gone, and Franklin standing next to my bed.

Really?

I don't consider myself too vain, but I know I looked terrible. My makeup from the night before had not been washed off, so I probably had mascara on my cheeks, my hair was a mess, my mouth tasted like the Sahara Desert, and I was wearing a faded blue, flower-print hospital gown.

Did they want me to relapse?

"I'm sorry to bother you," Franklin said, "but I need to talk to you about what happened last night."

I sighed and then worried if he could smell my breath. Well, he didn't fall over dead, so I guess he couldn't.

"Why, so you can blame me for it?" I asked. "Oh, and by the way, I'm feeling better. Thanks for asking."

I figured if I couldn't be cute, then at least I could be bitchy.

Then he sighed and shook his head. "I'm sorry," he said remorsefully. "I'm glad you're feeling better. I heard that Ida's doing better this morning too."

"She is?" I asked, feeling relieved. "I've been so worried…"

He nodded. "Yeah, I figured you would be," he said.

"Why, because it was my fault?" I countered quickly.

"No," he said immediately. "Because that's the kind of person you are, you've always been, worried about other people."

I calmed down.

"Thank you," I replied apologetically. "And thank you for letting me know about Ida."

He shuffled from one foot to another and then shrugged. "I'm sorry. I still have to ask you about last night," he said. "For the record."

"Whose record, Franklin? The Mississippi Bureau of Investigation or the Sons of Mississippi?" I asked, meeting his eyes.

He didn't flinch, didn't lower his eyes, but met mine straight on. "The Mississippi Bureau of Investigation," he said. "I don't work for the Sons of Mississippi."

"But you did want the files that were associated with them from the Anderson place?" I countered.

He nodded. "Yeah, the Congressman asked me to see if I could locate them," he admitted. "But he just said they were old files that were no use to anyone else."

"Well, now I guess we'll never know," I replied. "Since both places have been torched."

"So, the fires, they weren't an accident?" he asked.

"Well, I suppose if you think someone barricading the door from the outside while it's obvious that there were people inside the house and then lighting two separate buildings on fire could be considered an accident, it could be considered an accident," I replied sarcastically.

"They barricaded you in?" he gasped.

I nodded. "My car was in the drive," I said. "The lights were on in the house. Whoever did this, knew I was inside."

"And the first building didn't catch the second building on fire?" he asked.

"No. Maribelle told me that she could see the diner burning through the trees when she got out," I said. "They were set on fire separately."

"That's…that's not what I was told," he stammered.

"Yeah, and I wondered who told you the other version," I countered.

He pulled up a chair and sat down, then ran his hand through his hair. "Are you sure? Are you really sure?" he asked. "I thought they were good people. I thought they were harmless."

"The Sons of Mississippi?" I asked.

He nodded and then looked up at me. "Could they have really done this?"

"When did you get the call?" I asked. "About the fire?"

He picked up his phone and scrolled through it. "About eight o'clock."

"Georgia didn't call 911 until 8:15. You can check that with the emergency operator," I said. "Ida and I didn't get out until closer to 8:25. How could they call you about the fire at eight?"

He looked shaken and he inhaled sharply. "They couldn't have unless they started it," he admitted. "Or knew who started it. I can't believe that I fell for them. I can't believe they were willing to kill you."

I thought about Bud and how he hadn't realized who they were when he joined them. I wondered if Franklin was in the same boat. I hadn't seen his name in the portfolio. What if he was just as in the dark as Bud had been?

"Franklin, they did this, and they've done even more," I said.

Now his face was filled with resolve.

"Show me, Louella Jo," he insisted. "Show me some proof, so I can arrest them."

I really felt that he was being earnest, that this wasn't some kind of an act to get me to believe him. Maybe it was time to trust him.

"Okay, I'll call you once I'm released," I said. "And I'll show you what I know."

He stood up and nodded. "Thank you," he said.

"For what?" I asked.

"For trusting me," he replied. "I know I haven't acted in a way that deserves that."

I smiled at him. "But you're willing to believe me now," I said. "And it'll be nice to have you on our side."

Chapter Fifty

"Oh, sweetie, you look terrible," Kyle exclaimed as he walked into the hospital room a few minutes after Franklin left.

Thanks. Thanks a lot.

"That washed-out blue gown does nothing for your complexion, your hair is a rat's nest, and you have dark circles totally encompassing your eyes," he continued.

"Did someone send you in here to cheer me up? Because if they did, they asked the wrong person."

He grinned at me and held up an overnight case. "As long as you're sassy, I know you're feeling okay," he said. "And lookie, I brought you clean clothes, toiletries, and make-up."

"Okay, you're forgiven," I replied, slipping out of the bed my hand clasping the back of my gown and my other hand reaching out for the overnight case. "Now, if you can convince them that I should be released…"

Kyle nodded. "Consider it done," he said. "I'll turn the full Kyle charm on, they won't be able to resist. And then I'll take you home, so you can rest."

I decided not to argue…yet. And once he left, I hurried to the bathroom to shower so I could feel human again.

Twenty minutes later, I felt like a new person when I opened the bathroom door and Kyle was sitting in the chair next to the bed.

"Now, that's the L.J. we all know and love," Kyle said with approval.

"Thanks," I said, zipping up the overnight bag now filled with my dirty clothes. "So, what's the good news?"

"You're outta here as soon as the doctor signs the papers," he said. "So, we've got about a twenty-minute wait."

I started to argue, but he lifted his hands to stop me. "And in the meantime, we can go over to Ida's room and visit with her."

"Really?" I exclaimed. "Oh, that's wonderful! I've been so worried."

"I thought so," he said. "So, gather up your things. Your carriage awaits."

"Carriage?" I asked.

"Wheelchair," Kyle explained, pointing out the door to the hallway.

"I don't need..."

"Hospital policy," he interrupted. "Sorry, there was nothing I could do about that one."

"Fine," I said, grabbing my purse and phone. "I guess I'm ready."

I climbed into the wheelchair, piled my overnight case and purse in my lap, and Kyle wheeled me down to the end of the hall. He knocked on the slightly ajar door.

"Come in," Ida called in a surprisingly strong voice.

"I brought you some company," Kyle announced as he wheeled me in.

"Oh, Louella Jo," Ida cried. "It's so good to see you. I was so worried."

I slipped out of the wheelchair and hurried over to her bed. The top of her head was wrapped in bandages and her arms were covered with light gauze. "How are you doing?" I asked, afraid to hug her for fear of hurting her.

"You better give me a hug," Ida said, reading my thoughts. "My head aches and my arms are tender because of the burns. But the rest of me can get hugged."

I carefully embraced her, tears filling my eyes as I felt a combination of relief and regret. "I'm so sorry," I whispered, my throat thick with emotion.

"Sorry?" Ida replied. "Sorry for what? You came back and found me. You saved me."

"But if I hadn't..."

"If you hadn't what?" Ida demanded kindly. "It was my idea remember. I'm the one who said I had a key. I'm the one who suggested we go. I'm the one who overruled you when you said no."

I didn't really know what to say.

291

"Besides," she continued. "If we hadn't gone, I wouldn't have been able to save Grammy Anderson's recipe box. It would have been destroyed in the fire and that box is like a family heirloom."

Then I smiled. "I heard they had to pry it out of your hands," I teased.

She nodded and laughed. "I know I wasn't thinking clearly," she said. "But even half-delirious, I knew what was important."

"Have you looked through it yet?" I asked.

She shook her head. "No, I'm not really up to it yet," she said. "But I plan on doing it as soon as my arms aren't so sore."

I could see that even our short visit was tiring her out. "Well, I look forward to tasting some of Grammy's recipes," I said.

Ida grinned. "Don't you worry," she said. "Once I'm out of here, I'll be cooking up a storm." She glanced around me to Kyle. "And you'd better be doing extra exercising because I plan on cooking for you too."

"Girl, I love me some southern cooking," he replied, as he came over and kissed her forehead. "So, you better just concentrate on getting better."

She yawned and then nodded. "I will," she said.

I kissed her cheek, then stepped back. "You get some rest," I said. "And we'll be back to visit you soon, hear?"

"Yes, ma'am," she said, yawning again. "I will."

Chapter Fifty-one

"We need to talk," Kyle said once he'd helped me into his car and then gotten in on the driver's side.

"Okay," I said with trepidation. I hated when conversations started with those words. It was rarely good news.

He started the car, pulled out of the hospital parking lot, and headed toward our house. "I am so sorry," he said, his voice breaking. Then he shook his head as emotion overcame him.

"Just sorry," he whispered.

"For what?" I asked, tears appearing in my eyes in sympathy.

He took a deep breath and waited a moment before answering. "For leaving you," he said. "For being upset with you. For everything wrong I did yesterday."

Sometimes I think that without guilt, we wouldn't have anything to talk about.

"You didn't leave me," I said. "I did something wrong, and you were angry. You were justified in being angry. And, when you found out the truth, you needed some time with Bud to sort things out. I also put you in that situation. So, there is nothing for you to be sorry about."

He glanced over at me, then back to the road. "Then why am I feeling so bad?" he asked.

I grinned. "Because we think we can control the universe and when something bad happens we are sure we should have been able to stop it someway," I replied.

He glanced over at me again and there was a hint of a smile on his face. "How'd you get so smart?"

"Momma pretty much laid down the line last night when I was feeling guilty for what happened to Ida," I said, then I shrugged. "I guess I actually listened to her."

"What happened?" he asked.

"Ida and I were in the kitchen, searching for the files when Maribelle came rushing in to tell us the place was on fire. Then, when we tried to escape, we discovered the front door was blocked from the outside."

Kyle swore.

"I agree," I said. "So, I remembered the mudroom and we all hurried back there – me leading the way. The backdoor was boarded up, but there was an ax next to the door. I lifted it, swung, and pretty much nothing happened."

"We've got to get in you into the gym for arm days," Kyle said.

"Then Maribelle picked up the ax, swung it, and broke enough down so Georgia and Kasey could fit through."

"Maribelle might be skinny, but she is tough."

"Right?" I agreed. "But we needed a little bigger opening for Ida. So, Maribelle kept swinging and I turned around for Ida and realized she wasn't there. She got lost in the smoke. So, I found her in the pantry and pulled her out just as Maribelle broke down the door. But the influx of fresh air kind of fed the fire and there was an explosion."

"An explosion! I didn't hear anything about an explosion," he exclaimed. "You were in an explosion and I'm taking you home from the hospital." He shook his head. "Oh, no girl, we are turning this car around and going right back there."

"I'm fine," I said. "We were nearly out of the house when it happened. I just got hit by flying debris."

"Are you sure?" he asked.

I nodded. "Really sure," I said.

"Well, if you're sure because Maribelle called me and told me she didn't see any reason to close the salon today," he replied.

"Except that, I texted her and told her to do it," I said.

He waved his hand in dismissal. "Oh, so what are you, the boss or something?" he teased. "We can handle it."

"Only on the condition that you treat all of those ladies to the best lunch money can buy," I said, knowing what battles I could win. "They've had a crazy couple of days."

"Oh, that's right, I heard about yesterday," he said.

"Right, I just told you about yesterday," I replied, a little worried about his cognitive functions.

"No, I mean about my appointments," he said. "I heard you took them all."

"Well, it was the least I could do," I said, then I smiled. "Besides, now you can take mine."

He met my eyes and shrugged. "And they will be so amazed by my skills, they'll want to become my customers," he threatened.

"That's a risk I'm willing to take," I said, "because all I want to do is get home and rest."

I slid my hand down between the seat and the door and crossed my fingers.

"Good," he said, as we pulled into the driveway.

"Because that's all you should be doing."

Chapter Fifty-two

I waited for five minutes after Kyle left for the station before I called Franklin. I wanted to be sure Kyle didn't circle back because he forgot something. Basically, I didn't want to get caught doing something I knew Kyle would disapprove of.

Van went out early on the boat, so I knew I had until noon to meet with Franklin and then get back to the house and pretend I'd been resting.

"Hello, Franklin?" I asked when he answered his cell. "I'm ready to show you that proof. You remember the Old Crenshaw Place, right?"

When he answered he did, I just told him to meet me there in twenty minutes.

I slipped out of the clothes Kyle brought and changed into jeans, a t-shirt, and some hiking boots.

"Where do you think you're going, young lady?" Momma asked, appearing next to me.

"I'm meeting Franklin," I said. "I've decided to take your advice and trust him."

Momma paused for a moment. "I don't really recollect giving you that specific advice," she mused.

"Well, you must have, because I'm doing it," I replied easily. "He visited me at the hospital this morning and I think he finally realized the Sons of Mississippi are not as altruistic and innocent as he wanted to believe."

"Well, good," Momma said, still sounding unconvinced. "So, where are you going to meet him?"

This time I paused.

"Don't you even try lying to me," Momma immediately countered.

"At the Crenshaw Place," I said with a sigh. "I'm meeting him in twenty minutes."

"What!" she exclaimed. "Are you out of your mind? You can't go into that building again. You know what happened to you last time."

I shook my head. "Momma, you didn't raise an idiot," I said as I hurried out of my room and down the stairs. "I'm not going into the building; I just want to show Franklin what's in the pit in front of the building. I have a sneaking suspicion that there's more than Deputy Hill in that pit."

My keys were laying on the floor, just under the mail slot in the front door. Maribelle was kind enough to drive my car back here and then drop off my keys last night. I picked them up, along with my purse and phone, and headed out the door.

"I'm going with you," Momma said.

"Okay," I replied quickly. Actually, it was a relief that I wouldn't have to face driving up that long driveway alone.

"You're still not too sure about this, are you?" Momma asked, sliding through the passenger side door.

I shook my head. "No, I'm really not," I admitted. "I'm not too sure about a lot of things lately. But I also realize that in order to take this organization down, I need to have as many people on my side as I can."

I turned the car on and slowly backed out of the driveway.

"And you're sure you can trust Franklin?" Momma asked. "You're sure this isn't a trap."

I thought about her question for a few moments as I drove out of town toward the old mansion. I thought about Franklin's face when I told him we were barricaded in. I thought about the look in his eyes when I told him that Georgia hadn't called 911 until fifteen to twenty minutes after he'd received a call about the fire. I don't think he'd changed that much from our high school days together that I couldn't detect that he was trying to pull one over on me.

"My gut tells me that I can trust him, Momma," I finally answered.

"And the reason you're doing this while Van is out on the boat and Kyle is busy at the salon?" she asked.

Okay, that was a fair question. One that I needed to ask myself.

Why now?

303

Why by myself?

I glanced over at Momma, then shook my head. "Okay, I don't know if you can understand this," I said. "And I don't know if I exactly understand this myself. But I feel that I need to do this by myself because I need to not rely on others when I have to do hard things. I'm feeling like I could really get used to other people handling the hard things for me and me standing back and letting them."

Momma nodded slowly.

"You know, like having a bunch of knights in shining armor at my beck and call..." I continued.

"But you need to slay the dragon yourself," Momma added.

I nodded enthusiastically. "Yes. Yes, that's it exactly," I replied. "I need to slay the dragon. I need to be courageous. I need to rely on myself, so I can prove to myself that I can do it."

I took a deep breath and exhaled slowly, relieved to have figured that out. Then I smiled and turned to

Momma. "Besides, Franklin is going to meet me there in the middle of the day. So, what could possibly happen?"

Chapter Fifty-three

I couldn't bring myself to take the route that brought me up alongside the house, so I took the original back road that Van and I used the first time we visited the old house. I pulled the flashlight from the trunk, shoved my phone and keys into my pockets, and headed toward the narrow deer path.

"Why do you need a flashlight?" Momma asked as she glided alongside me. "It's the middle of the morning."

"Because the pit is deep and dark," I said. "And I want Franklin to be able to see the body or bodies inside it."

Momma shivered. "Well, that wasn't the answer I wanted," she replied. "How come you were able to see them last time."

"Because Deputy Hill appeared as a ghost to me," I said. "And believe me, it wasn't a pleasant experience."

I pushed aside a branch and held it for Momma, but she just moved through it and smiled. "Thanks anyway," she said with a grin.

I could see the boarded-up attic windows over the tree line and felt a cold chill run down my spine as I remembered my last encounter in the building. I stopped in my tracks and just stared at the building.

"Are you sure..." Momma began.

I took a deep breath and pushed my fear away. "I can do this," I said both to Momma and myself. "I need to do this."

I moved through the brush again, pushing spiderwebs and thorny branches to the side as I clomped forward toward the house. When I was about twenty yards from the house, I heard another car approaching from the opposite direction. Franklin must have taken the more direct route.

Once I cleared the brush and stood on the edge of the overgrown lawn, I could see Franklin standing next to the house in his uniform. I waved at him, and he smiled and waved back.

"This is creepier than I remembered," he said, walking toward me.

"You don't know the half of it," I replied.

He studied me for a moment, his face somber, and nodded. "Tell me," he requested.

Well, it was now or never, I guess.

"When I got home for Momma's funeral, Deputy Hill came to my house," I explained. "He was looking for a card file Momma had kept on her clients. A file that had notes on the things they'd discussed as they were getting their hair styled. The night of the funeral I went to the salon to look for the card file and I found it. While I was there, someone broke into the front of the salon. I didn't hang around, I just hurried out the back door. Deputy Hill came by early the next day, asking if anyone had stolen the card file."

"That's odd," Franklin said. "How would he know?"

308

"Exactly," I said. "Then I discovered that my house was bugged. So, we used it against them. Kyle mentioned that I'd received a box in the mail after I'd left for home. He said that he'd asked one of the girls at the salon I used to work at to mail it to me. Then I found out that the Deputy had gone to the post office and asked that any package for me be sent to the Sheriff's Department first."

"What?" he exclaimed. "What do they think..."

"Then I got a call in the middle of the night telling me that if I wanted to know who killed my momma, I needed to meet them at the beach."

"Tell me you didn't go," Franklin said.

I shrugged. "I needed to know," I said. "So I went, by myself, in the middle of the night. Deputy Hill was waiting for me. He told me that he had killed Momma and now he was going to kill me."

"What happened?" Franklin exclaimed.

"Deputy Hill was above me on the boardwalk, I was lower, in front of him, on the beach," I said. "I heard a motorboat, then I heard a shot, and Deputy Hill was dead. I dropped to the sand until I heard the boat speed away. I decided not to call the police because I didn't know who I could trust."

"I don't blame you," Franklin agreed. "But we never got a report that Deputy Hill had died. He was just reported missing."

I nodded. "Right," I said. "No one mentioned finding Deputy Hill's body. No one mentioned his death. Someone covered it up. But I know where they put him. And I'm pretty sure they've used the same location for other bodies."

"Where?" Franklin asked.

"Here, in a building used by the Sons of Mississippi for their initiation rites," I replied.

Chapter Fifty-four

"What? Initiation rites?" Franklin asked. "Where did you come up with that?"

"It's a long story," I replied, not sure I wanted to get into the whole paranormal aspect of this situation. One step at a time. "But when I was inside the building, I discovered a portfolio that had the signatures of the men who'd taken part in the initiation ceremonies."

"How did you even learn about this place? And about the ceremonies?"

"Ridge told me about it," I said, purposely neglecting to tell him it was after he was dead and deciding to leave Shelby Adair out of things for now. "He was bitter because he was never asked to be part of the inner circle."

"Inner circle?" Franklin asked. "Louella Jo, you've got to see that this sounds just a little crazy."

I nodded. "Yeah, I totally see that," I agreed. "Which is why I didn't trust you with this information at the beginning. But now, we've agreed to trust each other…"

He sighed and nodded. "Yeah, you're right. Sorry. I just… This is just…"

"Too weird for words?" I finished for him. "Tell me about it."

He smiled and slowly looked around the area. "So, Deputy Hill's body is buried somewhere on this property?"

"More like dumped than buried," I said. "There's a trap door under the portico. Come on, I'll show you."

We made our way to the house.

"Well, if I had to choose a place for dumping bodies, this would be my first choice," Franklin said, as we walked around the side of the house.

"Right? Isolated. Abandoned. Creepy. It fills all of the qualifications."

I stopped next to the edge of the trap door and ran my foot along the edge, pushing the dried leaves out of the way.

312

"What's this?" Franklin asked.

"The trap door," I said. "If you'll help me uncover it, then we can lift the door."

"Are you sure…"

"You need to see this," I said. "You need to know what's been going on."

We brushed off the loose dirt and leaves and uncovered the entire trap door. Franklin bent down, grabbed onto the newly exposed iron ring handle, and pulled. I wrapped my hands under the door once Franklin had lifted it several inches and helped to push it open. The door slammed onto the other side of the portico, sending leaves and dirt flying into the air.

"What was this?" Franklin asked, peering down into the depths of the hole.

"It used to be a secret way into the house," I explained. "They would catch slaves, put them in a carriage that had an opening on the floor, and then bring them here and unload them without being seen by anyone else."

"Lovely people, the Crenshaws," he said.

"Just about as lovely as the current owners," I replied.

I pulled out my flashlight and shone it down in the pit. I slowly moved the beam across the murky water until it landed on a large canvas bag. "I believe you'll find Deputy Hill in that bag," I said, looking up at Franklin. "And I think, once you get someone here to exhume his body, you're going to find more bodies, just like his."

"I can't believe they…"

A shot rang out and I felt something whir past my ear.

"Ooomph," Franklin gasped.

Blood was slowly spreading across the chest of his uniform.

"No!" I cried.

He looked down at blood in surprise and then looked up at me. "Run, Louella Jo. Run," he gasped. Then he dropped to his knees and fell forward into the hole with a splash.

314

"No," I cried, shaking my head in disbelief.
"No."

"Run!" Momma screamed. "Run now!"

Chapter Fifty-five

With tears blinding me, I stumbled backward, away from the hole, and fell down next to the house, shielded by the portico.

"You need to run," Momma said.

"I can't leave Franklin," I cried. "He might not be…"

Momma nodded. "I can check," she said softly. "You stay hidden."

Momma disappeared and I pulled out my phone. Pressing Van's number, I tried to catch my breath, but I kept gasping and shuddering as tears flooded my eyes.

"L.J.?"

Van's voice was like a shelter in the storm.

"Van?" I sobbed.

"Where are you? What's wrong?"

"Crenshaw Place," I stammered. "Franklin. They shot Franklin."

"Where are you?"

"Under the portico," I gasped. "Franklin fell…he fell…" The tears were heavier, and my voice faltered. I took another deep shuddering breath. "Oh, Van, he fell in."

"Where's your car?"

"On the side road," I said slowly. "The first place we parked."

"Have there been any more shots fired?"

I shook my head, then I realized that he couldn't see me. "No," I said, inhaling deeply. "No, just the one."

Momma reappeared next to me; her translucent eyes filled with tears. She looked down at me and slowly shook her head. I felt like I was breaking inside. Franklin was dead. My friend. My best friend from high school. Dead.

"What?" Van insisted. "What's happening?"

"Franklin…Franklin's dead," I sobbed. "Momma checked."

"L.J., you need to get out of there," he said urgently. "You need to use the trees and the brush for cover because there might be a sniper out there. But you can't stay where you are. You have no protection if they come for you."

I heard what he said, but it didn't register. All I could think of was Franklin lying in that hole.

"L.J.!" Van shouted.

I jumped. "What?" I gasped, my heart pounding.

"Get up and get out of there," he yelled. "Do you hear me?"

I nodded and pushed myself up onto my feet.

"You run in a crisscross pattern. You use trees and anything else to hide behind. You run faster than you've ever run in your life, hear?"

"Yes," I said. "Yes."

"You keep this phone connected to me," he said. "Now, take a deep breath."

I took a deep breath.

"Wipe those tears out of your eyes so you can see," he continued. "And run like your life depends on it because it does!"

Chapter Fifty-six

I ran as fast as I could, darting back and forth, hiding, sliding, falling, and then picking myself up. My heart was exploding against my chest because I was sure at any moment I would feel a bullet enter my body and they would win.

Sobbing quietly, I finally reached the shelter of the overgrown brush, and I took a minute to lean against a tree trunk and catch my breath.

"How are you doing?" Momma asked me.

I shook my head, unable to speak, and fought to fill my lungs with air.

"You're going to make it," Momma encouraged. "You're almost to your car. Once you're there, you're home free."

I pushed myself away from the trunk and shoved through the branches and spiderwebs towards my car. I didn't care what I had to go through, I just needed to reach my car. I tripped over an exposed root and stumbled

319

forward, but I caught myself before I fell to the ground by grabbing hold of a rough branch that scraped the palms of my hands.

I straightened and looked down at the blood seeping through the jagged cuts on my skin.

"How much blood?" I whispered. "How much blood will they spill?"

"What did you say, sweetheart?" Momma asked.

I turned to her, my fear morphing into anger. "How much blood?" I exclaimed. "How much damn blood do they want? How much blood will be enough?"

"I can't answer that," Momma said sadly. "I don't know if it will ever be enough."

The anger energized me, rage flowing through my veins. I stood up tall and ran the rest of the way to my car. I unlocked it with the key fob when I was a few yards away and then sprinted to the door. I slipped the key into the ignition, turned the car on, and threw it into reverse in a matter of seconds. I spun out of the drive as quickly as I could and soon I was on the highway, heading back into town.

"Van?" I called into my phone. "Van, are you there?"

"Yes," he replied immediately. "How are you doing?"

"Call the police," I breathed. "Call the police and let them know what happened to Franklin."

There was a long pause on his end of the line.

"What?" I asked. "What's wrong?"

"L.J., Franklin was the police," he said. "I'm not sure who we can trust to call at this point."

"What? They'll see his body. They'll know he was shot. They'll go after the Sons of Mississippi," I said, confused about Van's reaction. "Van, they killed him."

"L.J.," he said, his voice low and calm. "Where are you?"

"About ten miles from town," I said. "Why? What difference does that make?"

More silence, then a sigh.

"I have some thoughts about what happened today," he finally said. "And I wanted to wait until you were here, in person, before I mentioned them."

"No. Don't wait," I said. "Tell me now."

"Did you call Franklin and ask him to meet you at the Crenshaw Place?" he asked.

"Yes. I told him at the hospital that I would tell him about the Sons of Mississippi," I said.

"Right," he said. "And did you tell Kyle or anyone else that you were going to meet Franklin?"

"No. I didn't. I just called Franklin and met him there," I said.

"And what did you do there?" he asked.

"I parked near the old road, and he parked near the house," I said. "He walked over and met me in the front yard, then we walked over to the portico. We both brushed away the leaves and dirt. He picked up the door using the handle and I helped push the door open. Then, while I was pointing my flashlight down into the pit, someone shot him."

322

"And not you," he said.

"Right," I said. "Only Franklin."

"Could they have shot you?"

I shivered and thought about my position compared with Franklin's. Then I remembered hearing the shot rush past my ear. "Yes," I replied slowly. "Yes, they could have shot me."

"So, why didn't they?" he asked.

Chapter Fifty-seven

"I need to think about that," I replied slowly.

"Are you okay?" he asked.

I nodded. "Yeah," I said. "I just need to think, that's all. Can you…will you meet me at my place?"

"I'm already here," he said.

"Thanks," I replied, feeling a little less frightened knowing that he was waiting. "I'll talk to you in a few minutes."

I disconnect the call and drove in silence the rest of the way home. Why didn't they kill me? Why weren't there two shots instead of just one? Why not kill me instead of Franklin?

My head hurt by the time I pulled into my driveway. Van hurried down the steps and opened my door after I turned the car off. He helped me out of the car and then pulled me into his arms.

I allowed myself to absorb his warmth, his comfort, but only for a few moments. I stepped back and

324

met his eyes. "We need to figure this out," I said. "We need to call the police. We have to report this to someone."

He slipped his arm around my shoulders and guided me towards the house. "I agree," he said. "But I think we need to be careful about our next step."

I shook my head. "I don't understand," I argued. "Why do we have to be careful?"

Van waited until we'd entered the house and he'd shut the door behind us. Then he turned me to face him. "Because L.J., they could be framing you for Franklin's murder," he said.

"What?" I gasped. "What?"

"Think about it," he said. "You didn't tell anyone else you were going to meet Franklin. As a matter of fact, everyone thought you were home, sleeping. So, you established an alibi."

"But…"

He held up his hand to stop me. "Then you called Franklin and asked him to meet you in some out-of-the-way place," he said. "Your DNA and your fingerprints are all over the area, just like Franklin's. You both open up the trap door, you shoot him, he falls in, and then you call the police and tell them it was a sniper."

"But it was!" I yelled. "I didn't do that. I would never do that!"

"I know that. The people who know and love you know that," he said. "But, the Sons of Mississippi have people at all levels of government. They can plant evidence. They can hide evidence. If you report Franklin's death…"

"Which will also expose Deputy Hill's death," I said.

"And whoever else is buried in that pit," Van added.

"So, they killed Franklin to shut me up?"

"No, they killed Franklin because they are playing a game of chess and they just made a move to check you," he said. "You don't know who to trust. You don't know who to report this to. You don't know what they're going to do next."

"But what if Franklin was wearing a camera? What if he recorded…"

Van shook his head. "They will have already gotten rid of it," he said. "And probably planted a gun on the scene."

"But it wouldn't have my fingerprints," I said.

"You wiped it clean before you threw it into the pit with Franklin," he retorted.

It suddenly hit me. Van was right. They could do this. Not only could they kill Franklin, but they could also blame me for it. I felt sick to my stomach.

"I…I need to sit down," I stammered, stumbling toward the front parlor.

I sank down in a chair and just stared ahead.

What was I going to do?

How was I going to prove my innocence?

I turned to Van who had knelt down next to my chair. "How…" I breathed.

"I called D.C.," he said. "We need to have someone from the agency here in Julep to help with the investigation. That's the only way I can think of keeping you safe."

"But what about Franklin?" I asked. "We can't leave him there."

"I think if Franklin were here, he would insist that you protect yourself first," he said. "And that's what we have to do. We have to protect you."

Chapter Fifty-eight

I sat at my kitchen table, not listening to the conversation going on around me. My mind was filled with conflicting thoughts and basic disbelief. A man was dead. No, not a man, my friend, my very good friend was dead. His body was lying in a pit, a disgusting, water-filled pit, and there was nothing I could do about it because someone was trying to set me up.

How did that happen?

What happened to the law?

What happened to innocent until proven guilty?

What happened to truth, justice, and honor?

When did power and evil overrule good and right?

This is not the way it's supposed to happen. Good conquers evil. Honesty is stronger than deceit. Cheaters never prosper.

When did that change?

"L.J., did you hear me?"

I was startled into awareness when Bud called my name.

"I'm sorry, what?" I asked.

"How much of this conversation have you actually heard?" Kyle asked.

I sighed and shook my head. "Sorry," I replied softly. "I wasn't listening. What did you need?"

Bud reached over and enveloped my hands in his, his giant, work-roughened hand completely covering mine. "Listen, Louella Jo," he said gently. "I know this is hard. And I know that right now, it seems like your world has been flipped upside down. But we've got to work together, sweetheart. We've got to figure a way to keep you safe."

"But is that the most important thing?" I asked, confusion stirring my heart. "Keeping me safe?"

I glanced away from the table for a moment, just to gather my thoughts, then I turned back to them. "Isn't the most important thing making sure that Franklin's body is treated with respect? Isn't the most important thing

330

making sure that those people who did this are caught and punished? Isn't the most important thing ensuring that no one else dies?"

"None of those can happen if we don't keep you safe," Bud replied.

"Why?" I asked. "What's so important about me?"

Bud released my hand and leaned back against the kitchen chair so it squeaked with the pressure, and I wondered for a moment if it would crumble under his weight.

"Well, young lady, that's a very good question," he said with a slow nod. "They could have killed you. But they didn't. Why not?"

"Because finding both bodies there would have caused an uproar," Van said. "And there would definitely be an investigation."

"Yes, that's a good point," Bud agreed. "But why not before this? Why not kill her before this?"

"They tried," I said. "They tried locking me in the Anderson house when they set fire to it."

"But it didn't work," Bud said. "Right?"

I nodded. "Right, but not for lack of trying," I replied.

"How many times have they tried to kill you?" Bud asked.

I shrugged. "I don't know, maybe a couple of times," I said. "Deputy Hill on the beach, Crenshaw Place when I went there by myself," I paused. "Then there's Ridge, but that didn't count because it wasn't the Sons of Mississippi."

"Then there was the thing outside the cemetery," Van reminded me. "Whatever that was, it wanted you dead too."

"But, somehow, you were able to evade all of those attempts on your life," Bud said. "Don't you think that's unusual?"

"Not unusual," Kyle inserted. "Chosen."

"What?" Bud asked.

"Myrtle told her that she was the one, she was the key," Kyle explained.

"But the Sons of Mississippi don't know that," I argued.

"Maybe they do," Bud said slowly. "Maybe by escaping all of these attempts on your life, maybe by being able to overpower their demon, maybe by being able to outsmart them, they realize that they are up against more than they counted on."

"So, they want to take her out?" Van asked.

"They want to frighten her out," Bud replied.

Frighten me. They thought they could frighten me?

Well, you know, maybe during those first few days or even weeks, when all this was first happening. Maybe then they could have scared me away. But now, with all of the sacrifices others have made to help me stop them, sorry, I'm way too committed to stop now.

"Well, that's not going to happen," I said. "I'm not backing away."

"Good," Bud said with an approving smile. "Well then, let's put together a plan."

Chapter Fifty-nine

It wasn't officially a part of the plan. And actually, no one else at the table liked the idea, but I just couldn't leave Franklin in that pit. But I knew that I couldn't do it by myself, I needed a group of people with a specific set of skills.

"Welcome," Bea said, opening the door of the plantation and ushering me in. "We're all here and just waiting for you."

I gave her a hug. "Thank you so much," I said. "I can't tell you…"

"No, this is the right thing to do," she interrupted. "There's no need for thanks."

We walked through the front hall to the parlor where all of the women of the Book Club were sitting.

"Well met," Trudy said, dressed in a long, slim, black dress with long tight-fitting sleeves. She stood and walked over to me, placed her hands on my upper arms, and kissed each of my cheeks. "We are ready to help you."

"Thank you," I replied.

Clarise and Dottie were both dressed in black jeans and black turtlenecks shirts, Effie was dressed in a black tunic and black leggings, and Bea was dressed in a black pantsuit with her blonde hair tucked into a black stocking cap. I glanced at the mirror on the wall and saw, including my own black attire, that we truly looked like a modern coven of witches ready to go out and cast spells on unsuspecting victims.

"We look like…" I began.

"Spies!" Dottie said with a sparkle in her eyes.

Trudy met my eyes, a twinkle of mirth in hers, and nodded. "Exactly, Dottie," she said. "We do look like spies." She raised her hands over her head. "But we will begin with a blessing for protection. Come, form a circle."

We all formed a circle in the middle of the room and clasped each other's hands. I stood between Trudy and Clarise and as soon as I touched their hands, I felt a frisson of energy pass through me. But the energy wasn't jolting, it was empowering and invigorating. I took a deep breath and the air smelled like the atmosphere after an electric storm had just passed, filled with power.

"Sisters," Trudy began, her voice low and melodic. "Let us begin."

We all bowed our heads and closed our eyes.

"We ask for thy divine blessing this night," Trudy prayed. "That we may have protection as we go forth on a mission of mercy. We pray that the night will conceal us. We pray that our powers and gifts will aid us. We pray that those forces who stand against us will be stayed by thy hand. And we pray that the spirit of our friend will be welcomed to the place beyond this life and greeted by those who love him."

"And now, sisters," Trudy added. "We go forth with the conviction that we will be blessed."

We left Bea's house and divided up into two cars. I drove my car with Bea and Effie as passengers and Trudy drove her car with Dottie and Clarise.

337

"How do things look?" Bea asked Effie as I turned off the driveway onto the road.

Effie closed her eyes and concentrated for a moment. "I see three men," she said, opening her eyes and meeting mine in the rearview mirror. "They wait for us."

"I'm hoping that's Van, Kyle, and Bud," I explained. "They wanted to be lookouts for us."

Effie smiled and nodded. "Yes, their intentions were pure," she agreed. Then she closed her eyes again and I saw her shiver. "There is something evil there. In the house."

I felt goosebumps crawl up my arm, and I nodded. "Yes," I agreed. "There is something very evil in that house. Myrtle fought it the last time I was in the house. But I haven't felt its influence outside of the house."

Effie was silent for a few more moments and then she nodded. "It is within the walls of the house," she agreed. "We should be safe, but we must be cautious."

"Yeah," I agreed. "Really cautious."

Chapter Sixty

I really didn't want to lead all of us through brush and spider webs in the middle of the night, so I choose to use the long lane that led up to the side of the house. The road was rough, but it was passable, and soon we were parked near the portico.

The lights from my car shone into the area under the portico and I saw that the trap door had been closed. Someone had come after to set things right and, if Van was correct, to add more things to implicate me.

"The trapdoor is over here," I said to Trudy. "It's not hard to open."

"I think we should use our gifts as much as we can," Trudy said. "So, we don't leave trace evidence." She turned to Dottie and Clarise. "Would you two open the door?"

Dottie and Clarise held hands and concentrated on the door for a moment, then they stopped and turned to Trudy.

"There are many souls below," Clarise said, her eyes filling with tears. "Many who are confused and despondent."

"They want to be released, too," Dottie added. "They want to find peace."

I thought about Pammy Jo, I was sure she was down there, caught between the darkness and the path to the speakeasy. I wondered how many other young women were down there too.

Trudy turned to me. "What would you have us do?"

"What are the consequences of releasing them?" I asked. "Could harm come to Dottie and Clarise?"

"Most would seek the light," she said. "And their spirits would finally be at rest. Some might become more active, seeking vengeance on those who did this to them."

Yeah, I couldn't see a downside here.

"Please, as much as they are able, release the spirits who are down there," I said.

341

Dottie and Clarise nodded, clasped hands again, and a moment later the trapdoor levitated and fell open. But I wasn't prepared for the sound that erupted from the pit, a shrill wail, like the cry of a banshee, rose from the pit in a solid column of sound, represented by a coil of hundreds of translucent threads. Then, once it reached just past the height of the house, it split into hundreds of individual strands scattering in all directions, carrying the mourning cry of each spirit along with it.

It was a sound that tore at my heart. It was a sound beyond sadness, a sound beyond pain.

My phone rang. I looked down and saw it was Van, so I quickly answered it.

"Are you okay?" he immediately asked.

"Yes, we're fine," I said, still a little overwhelmed by the sorrow that hung in the air.

"We're coming up," he replied and disconnected before I could argue.

I turned back to the pit and saw that Clarise and Dottie were kneeling next to it and holding each other, as they sobbed together.

"Are they going to be alright?" I asked Trudy.

She nodded. "They are empaths," she explained, "So, they felt the grief of the spirits as they passed on. But soon they will feel the elation of the spirits as they reach the light, and their energy will be restored."

"I can help now," Effie said, walking over to the trap door. "Would you let me know who you need to have extracted?"

I pointed my flashlight into the pit and shined it on the still lifeless body of Franklin. Tears filled my eyes and emotion clogged my throat. "There," I whispered, barely able to choke out the word.

Effie closed her eyes again and concentrated. To my astonishment, Franklin's body started to slowly rise from the bottom of the pit and levitate toward the surface.

"Lay him on the tarp over here," Van called from just a few feet away.

Kyle, Bud, and Van unrolled a large black tarp and laid it alongside the pit, and Effie carefully moved Franklin's body to its center.

"I wouldn't have believed it if I hadn't seen it with my own two eyes," Bud said in astonishment.

"Hello, Bud," Effie said with a tired smile once she opened her eyes. "Nice to see you."

"You too, Miss Effie," he replied. Then he looked down at the body. "Nice work."

"Thank you," she said, then she sighed. "I really need to sit down now."

Trudy placed her arm around Effie's waist and helped her back to my car.

"What happened?" Bud asked.

"Psychic gifts aren't free," Bea said. "When you do something like this, it takes a toll on your body and your spirit."

Kyle and Van wrapped Franklin's body up and gently carried him to Van's truck.

"We should go now," Dottie said, coming up beside me. "Someone's coming."

With gloved hands, Kyle and Van closed the trap door as the rest of us moved toward our vehicles. But Trudy stayed behind until they closed it, then she lifted her hands and spoke softly. Suddenly, leaves and dirt danced across the ground and covered the trap door.

She turned and smiled at me. "All as it should be," she said, then hurried to her car.

"All as it should be for now," I repeated softly. "Then, all as it must be eventually."

Chapter Sixty-one

Franklin's funeral at the small cemetery on
Abernathy property was private and peaceful. A small,
unblemished piece of granite marked his gravesite until
we could legally put his information on it. But my heart
was at peace, and I hoped that Franklin's spirit was at
peace too.

I stood by the grave as the others walked away,
back to the plantation where Bea had prepared a luncheon,
of course. I just needed to have a private moment to say
goodbye.

"Franklin," I whispered. "I'm so sorry. I'm not
only sorry that you were killed while you were just doing
what you believed was right, but also because you died
just as we were becoming friends again. You were my
best friend in high school. You made my life bearable.
You made me laugh. You helped me to see the absurdities
in life. You saved me."

Tears clogged my throat and fell from my eyes, and I impatiently wiped them away with my sleeve. "I'm so sorry," I repeated.

"You saved me, Louella Jo." I heard his voice in the whisper of the wind and felt his presence next to me. *"You saved me."*

Then his voice, as well as his presence, was gone.

I hope that meant he was on his way to the light. I hope that meant he didn't have any unfinished business, that once his body was laid to rest, he could rest too. He didn't need to stay around and avenge his death; he knew that I would do that for him.

I laid the small bouquet of blue forget-me-nots I'd gathered from Myrtle's garden on the fresh dirt and took a deep breath. "Rest in peace, my dear friend," I whispered, then I stood and walked toward the cemetery exit.

Chapter Sixty-two

"So, how are you doing, child?" Myrtle asked as she appeared next to me as I walked along the treelined path in the cemetery.

"I don't really know," I replied. "I'm filled with a mixture of emotion."

"Why don't you tell me about them," she offered. "Talking and sharing your burdens eases the mind."

I slowed my steps and tried to put my feelings into words.

"Sad," I said. "I feel sad that my momma is dead, that you're dead, that Franklin is dead, that Sheriff King is dead..." I shook my head. "Can you believe how many people have died in such a short time?"

"Why are you sad?" she asked.

"Because their lives were cut short," I replied. "They had so much more to live for."

"Are you sure?"

"What?" I exclaimed. "Of course I'm sure. Franklin was my age. He had his whole life…"

"But maybe that wasn't his plan," Myrtle replied. "All of us are on a journey through this life to learn, grow, and become the best people we can be. Then we move on, to the next stage of our existence. Every journey is unique. Every journey is individualized. Why do you assume they were all supposed to live beyond what they did?"

"I don't understand this at all," I said.

Myrtle chuckled softly. "Alrighty, let me explain it this way," she said. "Let's say life is like a cross-country trip on a train."

I nodded. "Okay."

"You get on at your station, right? Not before and not after, but at your station."

"Yes, I get on at my station," I said.

"But some people get on before you and some people get on after you, right?"

"Right."

"And some people get on at the same station you get on."

"Okay. Yes, that's right."

"And where do they get off?" she asked.

I shrugged. "Where they need to get off," I said, more than a little confused by this analogy. "At their departing station."

"But, if they get off before you, early, they're going to miss a lot of the scenery that you see on your trip," she said. "Won't they? Shouldn't they just stay on the train, to see it all?"

"Not if they'd miss their stop," I said. "Not if they'd miss their station."

"But the scenery," she countered.

"They'll see a different scenery where they're going," I said. "They don't need to go where I'm going."

"You're right," she said. "They don't need to go where you're going. They don't need to experience what you need to experience. They need to get on the train when they got on and get off when they need to get off.

350

Their journey hasn't ended, they're just not riding the same train anymore."

I turned to her. "Are you at peace?" I asked.

She smiled sweetly and nodded. "Oh, child, I am so at peace my heart could burst," she replied. "They call it heaven for a reason."

"Do you know where my station is?" I asked. "Do you know when I'm going to get off?"

"Do you mean, do I know when you're going to die?" she asked.

I nodded again.

"No, child, that is only for God to know," she explained. "But don't worry yourself none, because He loves you and He knows what's best for you."

"I don't know what to do next," I said. "I'm afraid I'm going to do something wrong. I'm worried that I might miss something. I'm feeling overwhelmed."

"Well, have you truly made up your mind about what you're going to do?" she asked.

I nodded. "I'm going to expose the Sons of Mississippi. I'm going to fight them."

"And how did you feel, in your heart, when you made that decision?"

I had to stop and think about it. How did I feel?

It took me a moment to analyze myself, then I smiled at Myrtle. "I feel at peace," I said, surprised as I said the words. "I feel calm, even though I'm not sure what I'm supposed to do next."

"That's good," Myrtle said. "That's perfect. Because what you do next is just step forward, one small step at a time, and have faith that you will be led to do what you need to do."

"But what about tomorrow and next week and next month and..."

Myrtle chuckled. "Child, one step at a time and one day at a time," she said. "The rest will take care of itself."

"But..." I began.

She laughed and began to slowly fade away. "One step at a time."

Chapter Sixty-three

I arrived at the plantation just as Van was running out the front door.

"What?" I called as I jogged toward him.

"The hospital called," he said. "Ida needs to talk to us, and she said it was urgent."

We ran to Van's truck and in a few moments, we were racing down the highway toward the hospital. Van's foot was a little heavy on the gas pedal, so we made it in record time. We jogged through the lobby and then caught an open elevator to Ida's floor.

We were out of the elevator before the door was completely open and jogging towards her room. My stomach was in knots because I was expecting the worst, so imagine my surprise when we walked into the room to find Ida laughing at the movie on TV.

She turned and smiled at us. "Oh, good, you're here," she said.

"They called us," I panted, working to catch my breath. "Are you okay?"

354

"They said it was urgent?" Van breathed, as out of breath as I was.

Ida put down the bag of chips she'd been snacking on and picked up the old card file box. "It is," she said. "I needed to show you what I found."

"If this is about a recipe…" I began, not pleased with the emotion rollercoaster she'd just put us through.

She shook her head as she opened the lid. "Nope, much better," she said. "I was glancing through the index cards and realized they were all catching on something on the bottom of the box. So, I pulled the cards out and found these taped underneath."

She pulled out two small, black objects and held them out to me.

"Thumb drives," Van said. "In the recipe box."

"I'd guess, knowing Grammy Anderson, that these must contain the files you've been looking for," Ida said.

"Of course," I replied slowly, as Grammy Anderson's words returned to me. "She kept referring to cooking up trouble or a recipe for trouble."

Ida nodded. "That's Grammy Anderson, always playing around with her words like that. She hid them with her most prized possessions, her recipes."

"I can't believe it," Van said. "I thought this information was lost."

"Thank you, Ida," I said. "You not only saved a family heirloom, but you also saved the day. These files might give us what we need to stop the Sons of Mississippi."

"I'm glad to be of help," she said.

Van's phone rang and he glanced at it. "Sorry," he apologized. "I really have to answer it."

"This is Abernathy."

I couldn't hear the other side of the conversation, but I could see by the look on Van's face, he wasn't too happy about what he was hearing.

"Here? Now?" he exclaimed. "How did… Okay, yeah, GPS." He sighed. "Yeah, well, there's nothing I can do about it now. Okay."

What in the world?

He hung up the phone and met my eyes. "Can we talk for a moment, in the hallway?" he asked.

"Sure," I replied. I turned back to Ida. "I'll be right back."

She smiled at me and picked up her chips. "Take your time," she laughed. "I'm not going anywhere."

I followed Van out to the hallway. "What's up?" I asked.

"Do you remember that I reached out to D.C.?" he asked.

I nodded.

"And do you remember the female agent I told you about?" he asked. "The woman who…"

He paused.

"Kind of soured you on relationships?" I finished.

He nodded. "Yes, her," he said. "I just found out…"

"Well, Vandergast Abernathy, as I live and breathe."

The sultry purr was emitted from a statuesque redhead who looked like she'd just stepped off the pages of Cosmopolitan. She was dressed in a short, black two-piece suit, green silk blouse that dipped low to show cleavage, and tall, spiked heels to show every inch of her gorgeous legs to full advantage. She walked like she was striding down the center of a catwalk, with the self-assurance and assertiveness that proved she was a woman who knew what she wanted and went after it.

I don't know, those aren't terrible traits. Maybe we could be friends.

"Hi, I'm…" I said, holding out my hand. But she brushed right past me, wrapped her arms around Van's neck, and plastered an opened-mouth kiss on his lips.

Yeah, this isn't going to end well.

The End

About the author: Terri Reid lives near

Freeport, the home of the Mary O'Reilly Mystery Series,

and loves a good ghost story. An independent author,

Reid uploaded her first book "Loose Ends – A Mary

O'Reilly Paranormal Mystery" in August 2010. By the

end of 2013, "Loose Ends" had sold over 200,000 copies.

She has nineteen other books in the Mary O'Reilly Series,

and books in the following series - "The Blackwood

Files," "The Order of Brigid's Cross," and "The Legend

of the Horsemen." She also has a number of stand-alone

novels and short stories.

Reid has enjoyed Top Rated and Hot New Release

status in the Women Sleuths and Paranormal Romance

category through Amazon US. Her books have been

translated into Spanish, Portuguese, and German and are

also now also available in print and audio versions.

Reid has been quoted in several books about the

self-publishing industry, including "Let's Get Digital" by

David Gaughran and "Interviews with Indie Authors: Top

Tips from Successful Self-Published Authors" by Claire

and Tim Ridgway. She was also honored to have some of

her works included in A. J. Abbiati's book "The

NORTAV Method for Writers – The Secrets to

Constructing Prose Like the Pros."

She loves hearing from her readers at

author@terrireid.com

Other Books by Terri Reid:

Mary O'Reilly Paranormal Mystery Series:

Loose Ends (Book One)

Good Tidings (Book Two)

Never Forgotten (Book Three)

Final Call (Book Four)

Darkness Exposed (Book Five)

Natural Reaction (Book Six)

Secret Hollows (Book Seven)

Broken Promises (Book Eight)

Twisted Paths (Book Nine)

Veiled Passages (Book Ten)

Bumpy Roads (Book Eleven)

Treasured Legacies (Book Twelve)

Buried Innocence (Book Thirteen)

Stolen Dreams (Book Fourteen)

Haunted Tales (Book Fifteen)

Deadly Circumstances (Book Sixteen)

Frayed Edges (Book Seventeen)

Delayed Departures (Book Eighteen)

Old Acquaintance (Book Nineteen)

Clear Expectations (Book Twenty)

Breakaway – A Mary O'Reilly Lost Files Book

Finders Mansion Mystery Series

Maybelle's Secret

Maybelle's Affair

Mary O'Reilly Short Stories

The Three Wise Guides

Tales Around the Jack O'Lantern 1

Tales Around the Jack O'Lantern 2

Tales Around the Jack O'Lantern 3

Auld Lang Syne

The Order of Brigid's Cross (Sean's Story)

The Wild Hunt (Book 1)

The Faery Portal (Book 2)

The Blackwood Files (Art's Story)

File One: Family Secrets

File Two: Private Wars

PRCD Case Files: The Ghosts Of New Orleans -A Paranormal Research and Containment Division Case File

Eochaidh: Legend of the Horseman (Book One)

Eochaidh: Legend of the Horsemen (Book Two)

Sweet Romances

Bearly in Love

Sneakers – A Swift Romance

Lethal Distraction – A Pierogies & Pumps Mystery Novella

The Willoughby Witches

Rowan's Responsibility

Hazel's Heart

Catalpa's Curse

Agnes' Answers

The Shear Disaster Series

BlowOut

Foiled

UnderCut

Made in the USA
Las Vegas, NV
07 June 2022

49932145R00203